HIGGINS HOTEL

HIGGINS HOTEL

CARLA COFFMAN

Auctorem House
276 5th Ave, Ste 704-2591
New York, NY 10001
www.auctoremhouse.com
Phone: 1 888-332-7718

Published by Auctorem House: 03/18/2025

ISBN: 978-1-965687-34-5(sc)
ISBN: 978-1-965687-35-2(e)

Library of Congress Control Number: 2024924998

CONTENTS

CHAPTER 1

"You've never seen my bad side," he said.

How strange that he thought I was seeing his good side, but be that as it may, I'll begin.

Jack Higgins hadn't aged well except that he still had an exceptional physique for a man of sixty-seven and the stamina of a Pamplona bull. Boxing had done a number on his face, but his wife was still beautiful, and he had plenty of money. He was generous to a fault. Thanks to his childless Aunt Lucy, a wealthy widow, he inherited some prime real estate including Jack's Gym and Higgins Hotel when he was still in his thirties.

Business was good, but lately Jack had begun sharing space in the crime section of the paper with a bookie named Chuck Floyd, and his wife hauled-ass to Florida to be with her parents and their daughter, Nicki. Affectionately known as Booboo, his wife ran the hotel, and Jack had the gym. She usually went to Florida for a month or so, but this time she left before Thanksgiving and didn't have any definite plans to return, she said.

Jack visited the family once during the Daytona 500, but that was the extent of their family gathering since she'd left back in November.

Jack really wasn't much of a family man. His passion was Jack's Gym and coaching boxing.

He usually had breakfast at the hotel and sometimes even spent the night there leaving off to the gym. He enjoyed the company of men, especially Chuck Floyd. Not that he was ACDC, but there's nothing strange about that, he thought. Chuck was a Golden Glove's champion and, also, a hell of a bowler, and took them to win the national bowling tournament in Las Vegas the previous year.

With Booboo in Florida Jack began to feel like an orphan in his own establishment. He worried that she wasn't going to come back. It was not bad enough that he was accused of racketeering, but now she had deserted him. He sat at the counter for breakfast early that morning glancing at the newspaper and thinking of strategy to improve his position.

"Damn Booboo. I'm going to have to put my foot down," he said.

As he consumed his usual eggs and bacon with biscuits and gravy breakfast, the waitresses became engaged in a lively discussion. They were used to Jack eating there and talking to himself occasionally and hardly paid him any mind. This particular morning the gossip was flying. His ears perked up as he overheard a couple waitresses laughing together.

"Can you imagine? Blossom bent over the bed and Jeff on top of her, and he said 'I'm changing a lightbulb'. John said 'well I think the lightbulb is up there."

"Susie is mad as hell," the other waitress said. "She'll kick Blossom's ass."

Jack typically wouldn't have given it a second thought except that Blossom was the good-looking redhead and built like a brick shit-house. He listened, not quite sure which one was Susie, but he knew Jeff and John in maintenance. Jack drank a second cup of coffee and made up his mind to call Blossom into his office for a chat.

He sat at the desk usually occupied by Booboo looking down at Blossom's personnel file when she came in and quietly sat down across from him. Her heart was pounding. She couldn't afford to lose her job right now. She knew everyone was talking about her and Jeff, but it was just Jeff horsing around. Now Susie was pissed at her and possibly she was about to be fired all over Jeff's ignorant bullshit she silently fumed.

"Blossom," Jack said still looking down at her personnel file. "I see you graduated from college with a degree in Human Resources Management."

"Yes," she said.

"My wife has been spending a lot of time in Florida and hasn't been carrying the work load to which I've become accustomed. I just don't have time to watch everyone around here the way I should. I need someone to take care of things, to supervise. How would you feel about filling her shoes?"

He shook his head in exasperation and took a deep breath then looked up and made eye contact with Blossom. Her worried expression changed to relief mixed with disbelief slightly suspicious in a way that made Jack smile. When she grasped that he'd just offered her a job she flashed him back a big smile, and he nearly creamed his jeans.

"Can you do it?" he asked.

"Are you kidding? I'd love to," she said.

"I'll give you a twenty percent raise for the first couple months, then we'll see," he said and closed the file.

"Thank you, Mr. Higgins," Blossom said gratefully.

"You can use this office. Be here at nine in the mornings. If I'm not here, call me at this number. It's my private number so don't give it out to anyone. You will need to hire another housekeeper right away to take your place. And call me Jack."

He wrote his number down on a piece of paper and handed it to her. Never in his wildest dreams did he expect anything other than a little gratitude from her. It was simply a business decision, and the transition was surprisingly smooth.

After a few days Blossom mentioned that one of the conference rooms was practically never used and wanted to rent it out as office space to a real estate company. They worked out the details with the real estate company. and the glass wall next to the lobby was now populated rather than an empty shell. Then Blossom wanted to hire a Concierge. She could be very persuasive. Jack said to go ahead, but only part-time. He didn't care for her choice of concierge much as the guy was what Jack would call a 'fruit,' but people seemed to like him.

Blossom had initiative and drive, and after a few days Jack started to consider a proper salary for her. He hardly missed his wife anymore, but unfortunately she was still on the payroll and still a pain in his ass.

One afternoon Jack came back to the hotel and showered and shaved there, feeling a little horny. It had been weeks since he'd had sex with a woman. He came into the office and saw Blossom sitting there looking so fine in her pink bubble-knit sweater. He closed the door and locked it. Blossom looked up at him and without saying a word pulled her sweater up over her head revealing a large set of knockers spilling out over a pink lace bra. Her long red hair fell around her white shoulders as she slid off the sweater and tossed it. It was Jack's lucky day.

It was quick, but no one was complaining. Blossom was as surprised as he was.

"Damn, Jack, you are good," she said breathlessly.

"Did you think I wouldn't be?" he asked.

"I don't know what I thought," she said, "but you're good. I need a cigarette."

"Let's have a smoke then we can put our clothes back on. We wouldn't want to start a fire, now would we?"

"No, we sure don't want that," Blossom said and giggled.

But all good things must come to an end. One morning after Jack left for the gym his wife came back from Florida unannounced and made her appearance at the hotel. Blossom was sitting behind the desk making up the schedules, and she was startled to see her.

"What are you doing?" Mrs. Higgins asked standing at the door, dead in her tracks.

"Mrs. Higgins! Hello, nice to see you back. I'm the new Human Resource Manager," Blossom said.

"Really. Jack must have forgotten to mention that."

Blossom knew Mrs. Higgins could be a bitch sometimes, but she wasn't going to blow this job if she could help it. She smiled and shrugged her shoulders.

"Men," she said. "They can be so forgetful."

Mrs. Higgins' eyes seemed to go empty and black as she stood there glaring at Blossom. Booboo was petite and always dressed to the nines, tanned with blond hair swept back away from her face and possibly a face lift, Blossom thought.

"He's been busy training a new guy at the gym," Blossom said.

"I see. I'll catch up with you after I speak to Jack. We need to discuss a few things," she said and turned around and walked away.

Blossom dialed Jack's private number.

"Mrs. Higgins is back. Didn't you tell her about giving me this job?"

"I'll call you back," he said and hung up.

CHAPTER 2

J ack didn't want his wife showing up at the gym so he left and drove home. Her Lincoln was parked in the driveway when he got there. She was slamming cabinet doors when he walked into the kitchen.

"I guess I need to go to the grocery store," she said looking into the empty cabinets.

"No shit, Sherlock," he said.

"Did you promote one of the waitresses to Human Resource Manager?"

"She was in housekeeping," he said. "She has a degree in Human Resources. She's doing a good job."

"I'll be the judge of that," she said.

Jack really wasn't in the mood for her sarcasm.

"If you want to go to Florida and stay all winter, that's fine with me, but don't come back here handing out orders. Someone has to take care of business."

"Fine with me," she said. "I want a divorce, anyway. Then see how you like it."

Booboo could still see Blossom sitting at her desk looking like the cat that ate the canary… so smug. She was boss at the hotel, and that was one position she hadn't considered losing.

"I don't have time for your bullshit," Jack said. "I'll fucking kill you if you ever sue me for divorce, do you understand me? And if you can find someone else to eat your pussy, you have my blessing."

He made a sort of religious gesture crossing himself.

"You are disgusting," she said. "What kind of name is Blossom? Her parents must have been on drugs to name a kid Blossom. She'd have to be retarded to work for you, anyway."

"What the fuck is Booboo, Latin or something? Shut the fuck up."

"My name is Beulah, asshole," she screamed.

Jack had never hit her or any woman for that matter, but he pulled back his fist and punched her. She fell to the floor before she could blink. Jack leaned over her to see if she was alright, and she slapped him.

"You just wait until I tell our daughter what you did."

Jack got ahold of her arm and pulled her up standing her on her feet.

"I'm sorry. You know I never did hit you," he said gruffly.

"That's the last time you'll ever hit me, you rotten piece of shit," she said.

He shoved her back down onto the floor and stretched out on top of her unzipping his fly.

He yanked her pants off while she kicked and slapped at him. He turned her over and took her from behind with one arm around her waist and his other hand over her face. He bit down over her twisted hair and pulled the clip out and spit it across the floor. It slid across the tile making a sharp scratching noise as he moaned and fell to her side then pulled her into his arms. She was silent, unable to move as they lay on the cold kitchen tile.

"That's all you needed, a little attitude adjustment," he said in her ear.

Jack got up without any further comment as Booboo stayed on the floor with her thoughts going back to when they were in marriage counseling early on in their marriage. Jack had started accusing her of trying to poison him. He told her that he was having nightmares about it, and he knew she must want him dead. Finally, she convinced him to go with her for marriage counseling, but it didn't help. 'How is your sex life?' the lady therapist asked them. Jack said that their sex life wasn't any of her business. The session turned particularly nasty. Jack said he didn't remember something. Booboo was still on the floor trying to remember what it was that Jack said he didn't remember. She remembered it pissed her off, whatever it was. She said she didn't like cock for breakfast, and he called her a cold fish. Then it came to her. Oh, she thought, he said he didn't remember their wedding night. What an ass-hole. She got up off the floor and straightened her clothes and hair. She could hear Jack walking toward the door and ran to catch up with him. She caught the door before it closed and slipped off her wedding band and slung it at him as he got into his El Dorado. He spun out and left her standing there.

Booboo got ready to go get groceries while Jack returned to the gym. As she walked to her Lincoln she saw the sunlight reflect on her golden wedding band and walked over and picked it up. There were skid marks on it. She brushed it off and put it back on her finger and went to the grocery store. It was as though nothing had happened, as usual.

Blossom was a little shook up after Mrs. Higgins' visit and walked out of the office to the concierge and asked if Mrs. Higgins had stopped by.

"Who?" he asked and slid his Playgirl magazine out of sight underneath the desk calendar.

"Mrs. Higgins. She's back from Florida," Blossom said.

"No, I don't know her. Who is she?"

"She's Mrs. Higgins."

"Oh, you mean the boss's wife. Did she pack some heat?"

The concierge giggled, and Blossom laughed despite herself.

"Danny, we are expecting a lot of tourists for the Spring Regatta. Get some flyers to have available. Call the Chamber, they'll send you some, and ask for some new maps. These look ancient," she said picking up one of the maps and looking at it briefly.

"Okay. Thanks for the heads up. I'm always nice to little old ladies, but it doesn't hurt to know when the boss's wife is back in town, does it?" he said.

"She's not as old as Mr. Higgins, or at least she looks a lot younger. She is little, though, like a little toy poodle who has lost her plaything."

The concierge giggled some more.

"If Mr. Higgins comes back and asks you where I am, tell him I went to the market to get some more seafood. I won't be long."

Blossom left the office and walked up the street to Randy's Seafood Market. It was a chilly day, but it seemed like everyone had crawled out of their caves for some fresh air and sunshine possibly a little disappointed. She heard a whistle as she walked and glanced over to a new construction site and a crew of men working. The guys went a little crazy as she walked into Randy's Seafood Market.

It was quiet in there and smelled awful unless you just like the smell of salt and fish like Randy. He could dream of the waves hitting up against the side of his boat and pulling in a big one. His eyes brightened when he saw Blossom walk in.

"Hi, Ms. Blossom," he said smiling through a heavy black mustache.

"Hi, Randy. We need some more crabmeat and anchovies, please," Blossom said. "Give me ten pounds of crab and a pound of anchovies. People love our crab soup and those six-foot-long ham subs. My God, they are good with a swipe of anchovy!"

"Who buys six-foot-long sandwiches, the Greene Giant?" he teased.

"We sell them at the bar and take-out orders for parties. They're delicious."

"I'll have to try one. Can I get one for a discount?" he asked.

"Sure, if you want. Today?"

"I can pick it up around seven. It's poker night."

"Don't forget. It'll be ready by seven o'clock. I want a couple of those lobsters, but not right now, maybe this weekend."

"I won't name them, then," Randy said and watched her walk back up the street.

When Blossom got back to the hotel instead of going to her office she walked up the long hallway and into the kitchen with the seafood then placed the order for Randy's sub. She wrote up the bill with a discount. She knew this could very well be her last day being able to act authoritatively, and the taste of power was vanishing quickly from her mouth. No more walking up the street to order seafood, bossing people around or snooping into personnel files. Walking back to her office she could see through the glass into Jackson & Greenes Real Estate office. Everyone was busy talking on the phones. She noticed her new neighbor, Cindy, sitting at one of the desks talking on the phone. She lived in the same trailer park as Blossom and had a little boy. She knew Cindy was a real estate agent but didn't realize she worked for Jackson & Greene. She waited for Cindy to hang up the phone and walked over to her desk.

"Hi, Cindy. I didn't know you worked for Jackson & Greene."

Hi Blossom. I didn't know you worked here, either. Have you worked here long?"

"Three years," Blossom answered. "I was in housekeeping, but I was promoted to Human Resource Manager. I actually worked out the rental agreement with Jackson & Greene, and Mr. Higgins, of course."

"That's great! Congratulations. I love it here. It's much nicer than the office we had on D Street."

"What do you think about the new concierge?" Blossom asked.

"He wears lipstick, doesn't he?" Cindy said and giggled. "I don't know, maybe he'll grow on me. I was wondering, though, did you find someone to clean your trailer?"

"No, I'm afraid not."

"I could clean for you once a week, if you could kind of check to make sure Jason is home alright when I have to show property sometimes in the evening, maybe once a week."

"That wouldn't be a problem. Jason is a little cutie. Sounds like a good deal to me!"

"Would Tuesday be okay with you for me to clean?" Cindy asked.

"Yes, Tuesday would be good. You'll have to let me know when to check on Jason, though."

"I'm always home by seven, and he stays with my parents during the summer after school lets out, but I just like to make sure he comes straight home from school. He's a good boy and does his homework when he gets home."

"I understand. If I'm not at home when you come to clean there is a key under the mat, and you can let yourself in. I don't mean to be nosey, but are you divorced?"

"No. Jason's dad got killed in a car wreck before he was even born. We weren't married."

"I'm sorry. Are you dating anyone?"

"Sort of, I met a guy recently I've been seeing," Cindy said.

"If you need someone at night, if you just want to go out, I wouldn't mind watching him once in a while so you can go out."

"I appreciate that. Thank you," she said.

"I'll see you back at the ranch, Cindy," Blossom said.

Trailers are kind of like ranches, but not, of course. It was just an expression among the local trailer dwellers.

CHAPTER 3

Cindy was a pretty, slender blond and getting a lot of attention in the real estate business. She'd already sold a couple commercial properties. Plus she sold a duplex to a guy named Chuck and had fallen for him. Neither Cindy nor Blossom realized at the time that Cindy was seeing Jack Higgins' protégé. He and Chuck both coached boxing at Jack's Gym.

Chuck owned The Grill on the west side of town and took Cindy there for lunch when she was showing him properties for sale. Cindy cracked up at his silly jokes. They just hit it off immediately and had fun goofing off together.

"Cindy, it's for you, line one," the secretary said. "I think it's Chuck."

Cindy picked up the phone and said hello. She was all smiles as some of the other agents glanced at one another. Chuck asked her to come to his place for lunch.

"I'll be there in a few minutes," she said and hung up.

Cindy noticed the insurance guy was in the manager's office again. He was in Bob's office a lot, and another agent, Dottie, was always in Bob's office, too. You could see them, but you couldn't hear them. It looked like they were all the time plotting something. When Cindy walked past their little cubbyhole Bob's face made a startling transition into a rat-face and stared back at her with red beady eyes.

Cindy shook her head spontaneously, then swiped at a fictional fly and hurried out the door. That was weird, but he really does kind of look like a rat with that fuzz he calls a beard, she thought and brushed it off.

Chuck's Grill was kind of a greasy-spoon, but the food was good. It was just the guys who hung out there that were greasy, truck drivers and mechanics mostly, and a few girls who were obviously looking for a meal ticket. The juke box was playing when Cindy walked in, and Chuck was sitting at the corner booth. The smell of hamburgers and fries and chili hit Cindy in the face. She should have asked him to come to the hotel for lunch, maybe next time, she thought. Chuck was smiling at her and moved over for her to sit down in the booth beside him.

"Hotdogs are on the way," he said and put his arm around her.

Hillbilly-Dogs and Fries were the Special of the Day everyday. Cindy and Chuck snuggled together in the booth until their hotdogs came. Cindy was always hungry, and Chuck liked that about her.

"What would you like to drink?" the waitress asked.

"Root-beer for me, thanks," Cindy said.

Chuck was drinking a Bud. Cindy took a bite of the hotdog.

"Yum," she said.

"We use only the best wieners," Chuck said. "I'm sure you've heard of him, Oscar."

"Yes, I believe I have," she said and giggled.

"Do you like sports?" he asked.

"I play tennis sometimes and golf," she said.

"Not tricks, sports," he said, "like boxing and football."

"I used to like watching my grandpa shadow box," she said.

"See this nose," he said and pointed at his nose. "This nose has been broken four times, and it's still the best nose this side of Alabama."

"That's terrible," Cindy said. "I mean it must have hurt."

"I won every one of those fights. I break a rib, a rib for a nose."

"I believe you," Cindy said.

"I heard Booboo is back in town. I guess she was surprised to see Blossom sitting at her desk," Chuck said.

"Booboo?" Cindy asked.

"Mrs. Higgins, Jack's wife," he answered.

"I haven't met her."

"While she was in Florida, Jack hired a girl, Blossom, to take her place, and now she's back. I work out at Jack's Gym."

"Blossom is my neighbor," she said. "Small world."

"You need to come over and see my sketches," Chuck said.

"I would love to see your sketches," she said in eager anticipation.

Chuck was a classy, clean-shaven guy unlike Cindy's usual hippie types she casually dated from time to time. Chuck had neat, blond hair and dreamy blue eyes and dressed like a million bucks. He drove a vintage, red convertible and sent Cindy a dozen roses on Valentine's Day. She loved being with him and thought he could be the one.

CHAPTER 4

When Cindy came back from lunch a couple hours later the office got quiet when she came in and sat at her desk. She noticed the insurance guy was still in Bob's office and felt a shiver go up her spine. She'd almost forgotten about rat-face.

"What's going on?" Cindy asked looking around at the other agents sitting quietly absent of the usual buzz.

"Nothing," Helen said. "We were just talking about Mrs. Higgins being back in town."

"I haven't met her. I wouldn't mind going to the beach and getting a tan, though, sometime before I turn to ashes," Cindy said and looked down at her white arms and laughed. "I think Chuck and I are going to go to Nags Head for a couple days."

That seemed to get their attention, and Helen piped up.

"You better do it soon," she said and gave a nervous chuckle.

"Do you mean before I blow away? I hope so," Cindy said.

Helen's husband was a big executive at the power plant, and she was more sophisticated than most of the locals. Cindy couldn't quite read her, but she seemed nice enough even though they had nothing much in common.

"Well, no, I mean before the trial," she said.

"What trial?" Cindy asked.

"Chuck and Mr. Higgins were indicted for racketeering. You knew that, didn't you?" Helen asked.

Cindy felt like the breath had been knocked out of her.

"What do you mean? Ratearing? What does that mean?" she asked.

"Racketeering," John said and put his face down over his desk holding back laughter.

"They were indicted for racketeering," Helen said. "Don't you read the paper?"

"Just the For Sale section," Cindy answered slowly.

"You might get indicted, too," John said. "Have you ever heard Chuck and Jack talking together or on the phone?"

"No, but I don't eavesdrop like some people," Cindy said.

She thought John had overheard her conversation with one of her clients and called him trying to cut her out of the deal, of all the nerve. She looked into the manager's office and saw it again, the rat-faced Bob.

She jumped up and walked to Blossom's office. Maybe Blossom knew, she thought.

The others looked at each other and shrugged. Cindy walked down the corridor to Blossom's office and saw her sitting there idly.

"Blossom, do you have a minute?"

"Sure, come on in," she said.

"I just heard Mr. Higgins and Chuck were indicted for racketeering," she said.

Blossom was surprised to hear Cindy say that, even though she had known about it for some time.

"Well, yes, I've heard about it. I'm sure it's nothing to worry about, though. The feds harass them all the time. They'll end up having to drop it. They have no proof," Blossom said.

"I wonder why Chuck never said anything to me about it."

"Do you know Chuck?" Blossom asked.

"He bought a duplex from me. We've been dating," she said.

"Oh, right" Blossom said. "I wouldn't worry about it. Those guys get busted all the time. It comes with the territory."

Blossom was a little surprised that Chuck was seeing Cindy. He usually went for the more trashy types. Jack and Chuck bowled on Saturday nights, and Blossom was on a bowling league as well. The women were all crazy about Chuck.

"What territory?" Cindy asked.

"The Feds are always harassing hard-working people. You'd think they'd be arresting the lazy bums around here who won't work, the real bad guys," Blossom said.

"What is racketeering, what does that mean?" Cindy asked.

"Taking bets… gambling," Blossom said.

"That doesn't seem so bad. Can they put them in prison for that?" Cindy said.

"I don't think so. Jack and Chuck are good guys," Blossom said. "Don't worry about it."

"I have an appointment to show an apartment building this afternoon. It might turn into a sale, and I could be late getting home. Would you check on Jason this evening for me?" Cindy asked.

"I sure will. Good luck with that," Blossom said.

Cindy stopped at the ladies room before going back to her office where the other agents were chattering away again.

"I can't believe Cindy didn't know about that," Helen said.

"Me either," Irene said.

"She only reads the for-sale section," John said. "Maybe she didn't know."

"I feel kind of sorry for her," Irene said.

Helen wasn't as sympathetic and rolled her eyes. Irene's husband was an executive at the phone company, and she and Helen both got a lot of the transferred people coming and going and listed some of the nicest homes.

"Booboo said Jack isn't worried about it. She said she found her a boyfriend just in case, though. We go to the same beauty shop," Helen explained. "She said Jack told her if she can find someone else to eat her pussy to go right ahead."

Joe the insurance guy had been standing inside the door of Bob's office and walked out into the agents' office space.

"What the hell are you all talking about?" he asked.

"Booboo is back," Helen said looking down at her Multiple Listing Service book.

"I heard that Blossom and Jack have been locking the door and make noise, like this," Joe said in a hushed voice and then made some loud grunting noises. "Wonder what they could be doing."

"Probably rearranging the furniture," Irene said and rolled her eyes. "I don't see why you don't ask Cindy out, Joe. She's a pretty girl, and Lord knows Chuck is never going to settle down."

Joe wished he could get into Cindy's pants, but she hadn't given him the time of day. He walked back into the Bob's office. He and Bob were about to take off to the country club for a round of golf.

When Cindy came back to the office Bob and Joe and most of the agents had left. Thank God, she thought. She didn't want anyone overhearing she was seeing a rat and called her doctor to make an appointment.

"What's the problem?" the nurse asked her.

"I need a check-up. I'm seeing things."

She hadn't done LSD but once, and that was ages ago. Maybe it was a flash-back, she thought. Her appointment wasn't until the following week. She started to call back and say she needed an appointment right now, but convinced herself to calm down. She had to show an apartment building to Joey Romeo. She saw Romeo's Corvette pull up under the canopy. He got out of his Corvette and walked around to the other side of the car and opened the door for her.

"Thank you, Mr. Romeo," she said.

"How are you today, Cindy?"

"Funny you should ask," she said.

"Why? Have you been sick?" he asked.

"No, but I might have drank too much tequila this weekend," she said and laughed.

"I've done that a time or two. I switched to wine. It's a more mellow euphoria than liquor."

"What kind of wine do you drink?"

"French wine, Bordeaux," he answered. "Have you ever been to France?"

"No, but I've been to the Caribbean."

"When were you in the Caribbean?"

"A couple years ago. My friend Nikki and I took a cruise. I got seasick, but other than that, it was fun."

"How many islands did you go to?"

"Five, no, four, one we had to skip, St. Martin. I think there was some kind of unrest."

"Which was your favorite?"

"I liked Dominican Republic. It was wild. The Captain said something in French at the restaurant where we had dinner. I think it was something dirty. He was mad because they charged us $150 for a bottle of wine! It's right up here on the right," she said looking ahead at the apartment building.

"If it was good wine, maybe it was worth it. Is this the one?" Joey said and stopped in front of a big white brick building on the cul de sac.

"Yes, isn't it pretty? The location is perfect. See all the Magnolia trees," she said as he pulled over and parked.

They went inside and walked up and down the halls and up the stairs and down the stairs. Cindy unlocked the vacant apartment. Joey liked the looks of it, but he wasn't ready to sign. They walked back to the car and drove back quietly.

"Thanks for driving. Are you sure you wouldn't like to make an offer?" Cindy asked.

"Let me think about it," he said. "I heard you sold Chuck Floyd a duplex. He's been indicted for racketeering. Did you know that?"

"I just heard. I heard they don't have any evidence and will have to drop it."

"I heard it's going to trial."

"I don't know anything about it," Cindy said. "Don't wait too long if you want that apartment building. It'll go fast."

"I always sleep on big decisions," he said. "I'll call you tomorrow."

"Are you sure you want to take that chance, though? It might be gone."

"I know, but I'll have to sleep on it," Joey insisted.

CHAPTER 5

On Saturday Cindy still hadn't heard back from Mr. Romeo and decided to go to her folks for the weekend. Jason was their only grandson, and they doted on him. During warm weather they took him out with metal detectors to fairgrounds, old church grounds and cemeteries to hunt for treasure, and Jason loved it and already had a nice coin collection.

Cindy liked to visit her best friend Nikki who had just graduated from cosmetology school. They always had plenty to catch up on. Typically they were talking at Nikki's kitchen table, smoking a bowl, then out for dinner and a couple drinks. On Sundays sometimes they took their kids to the lake before she and Jason headed back. Nikki had a little boy Jason's age, but his dad got him every other weekend.

That particular night Nikki and Cindy met at their favorite restaurant for a nice steak dinner to celebrate Nikki's graduation. They sat at a table and ordered filet with baked potato and salad.

Nikki said she had lots to tell Cindy. She learned that the guy she'd been seeing during her cosmetology course was married, and not only that, the FBI called her about him.

"Remember George?" she asked.

"The one who followed you from class?"

"Yes. An FBI agent called and said I had better stay away from him. They said he's in the mafia!"

"What? The mafia?" Cindy laughed. "I guess they sucked him back in."

"I know. He said 'do you know George Barker is in the mafia. I said 'well, hell no, who am I, the gestapo?' I said I knew he was a liar, but that's more like a big fancy club with people swinging from the chandeliers than the mafia, though, right? I mean they cut off people's body parts. Can you imagine? So I called his house, and a woman answered the phone. I told her George said you guys were divorced, and she said, don't hold your breath, Sweetie, then she said, 'George told me he had a stalker, real snarly. I said he's the fucking stalker, sneaking around, following me to my car after school. Damn!"

"Dag, do you think he is?" Cindy asked.

"Let's change the subject," she said. "I got a shop rented"

"That's great, Nikki! Where is it?" Cindy asked.

"It's the old gift shop at the Motor Inn. They remodeled it with two stations. The girl that was going to do it backed out and moved to Texas! I open this coming Tuesday. I only have to pay ten percent of my pay for utilities. Don't look now, but see that guy standing at the bar beside of Dale. He's new in town. He's a reporter from Peterstown and got a job at the Chronicle."

Cindy gradually turned her chair around so she could get a look. The room was a little crowded, and the bar was full, but she recognized Dale and looked beside of him to the man who was standing beside him engaged in conversation.

"He's handsome. Is he married?" Cindy asked.

"No, he just got a divorce. I checked it out at the damn court house. Let's go over there and sit at the bar," Nikki said. "Okay?"

"Okay. Don't try to fix me up with Dale, though."

Nikki laughed. Dale was a decent guy and worked for the phone company, but he was a 'functional' alcoholic.

After finishing their meal they got up from the table leaving cash for their dinner and walked over to the bar which was on the way to the exit door.

"Hello, Dale," Nikki said and stopped glancing over at the new guy.

"Hello, girls," Dale said. "What are you girls in to?"

"Not too much. I haven't seen you for a while, Dale. Who's your friend?" Nikki asked sheepishly.

That was a lie. They saw Dale sitting at that bar practically every weekend.

"Oh, where are my manners," Dale said. "Nikki, this here is Frank Martin. Frank, meet Nikki Ditrapano and Cindy Bell."

Frank was probably Italian like her, Nikki thought.

"Have a seat, young ladies," Frank said and motioned for them to sit at the bar. "Get these girls a drink," he said to the bartender.

The bartender brought them their usual margaritas on the rocks, and Frank paid. "What do you girls do for a living?" he asked.

"I'm a hairdresser, and Cindy is a real estate agent," Nikki said. "I just graduated from hair-college."

"What a coincidence, I need a haircut," he said and swiped back his shiny black hair that fell below his collar around a square jawline.

Nikki was impressed. She hadn't seen a guy that good looking around there forever.

"I have some kick-ass Columbian redbud," Dale said. "Let's go out for a toke."

"Okay. Just a toke, though, then we'll have to be going," Cindy said.

Nikki finished her drink, and they all got up from the bar and walked out into the parking lot where Dale's van was parked.

"Did you ride with Dale?" Nikki asked Frank.

"No, there's my car," he said and pointed to a white Trans Am. Dale and Cindy sat in the front of Dale's van and passed around the joint a couple times to Nikki and Frank sitting in the back seat.

"Let's go to the Board Room," Dale said. "It's just a couple miles. They've got a good band, Crystal Cowboys."

"I haven't heard a good band in a long time. That might be fun… want to, Cindy?" Nikki asked coaxing her with her eyes.

Cindy wasn't overly enthused and crossed her eyes slightly.

"I'll take my car," Nikki said. "Cindy's with me. You guys can follow us."

They all got out of the van and Cindy and Nikki got into Nikki's Camaro, and Frank said he'd better drive, and they got into his Trans Am.

"It'll be fun," Nikki said as she and Cindy took off headed for the Board Room.

"I'm glad one of us is getting lucky," Cindy said.

"Ah, come on, the night is young," Nikki said.

CHAPTER 6

Cindy and Jason packed up late Sunday evening and headed back. Pulling into her driveway Cindy noticed Jack's El Dorado at Blossom's. Wow, they're getting brave, she thought. She and Jason hit the sack and woke up early the next morning. She made oatmeal and cinnamon toast for breakfast then took Jason to school and came back home.

Considering that she would have other agents riding with her looking at new listings that day she decided to clean out her car before going to the office. She noticed Jack walking to his car and pretended not to see him.

Jack got into his car and turned around to head back down the street past Cindy when he stopped suddenly and stared at the side of Blossom's trailer. Jack cursed and pounded his fist on the steering wheel turning red in the face.

Cindy was leaning into her vehicle taking out empty McDonald's bags and newspapers and stuffing them into a trash bag when Jack pulled up beside her and yelled at her.

"Cindy, if you can find out who did that," he said and pointed at Blossom's trailer, "I'll give you a thousand dollars."

Cindy had no idea what he meant but turned around and looked as he sped off like a bat out of hell. She stepped out where she could look and saw it, in big red spray-painted letters, WHORE, sprawled on the side of Blossom's trailer.

The neighborhood was still shaking off the Monday morning blahs and barely noticed Cindy standing there with her arms full of trash or Jack speeding down the street slinging gravel or even the big red bad word.

"What the fuck," Cindy said staring at it in disbelief.

Cindy wondered if Blossom knew what someone had done. It was still early, not yet nine o'clock in the morning, but she had to look at new listings this morning. It was her turn to drive so she decided to get going. She could stop by and see Blossom at the office later on in the day.

CHAPTER 7

It was a nice warm day to look at the new listings, and there were several to see with springtime listings coming in. Cindy drove Helen, John, and a new agent they just hired named Mark. Irene and Dottie always drove together. Mark lit up a joint, and he and John were smoking it. Cindy held up her hand no, then Helen reached out and took a toke off it. Mark wasn't bad looking and seemed nice enough, Cindy thought. He was married and had a couple teenagers in school.

"I'd better not go nuts and take off my clothes," Helen said. "If I do, you all will stop me, won't you?"

"Sure, we will," Mark said and did his impression of an evil laugh.

"I hate it when that happens. It's a nightmare," John said.

"Speaking of nightmares," Cindy said.

Apparently everyone already knew about her nightmare, Cindy thought.

"Not to change the subject, but what did Romeo think of the apartment duplex, I mean complex, Cindy?" John asked.

"He said he'd call me, but I haven't heard from him," Cindy said. "Did you guys show it yet?"

"Yes, but my guy said he didn't want it because it's HUD. I thought that would be a plus. I'm surprised someone hasn't already put a contract on it," John said.

Cindy slowed down and pulled over to the curb to see their first new listing of the day.

"There it is, 527 Beauregard. Does anyone want to see the inside?" Cindy asked.

"I do," Mark said. "I have a prospect that wants to duplex one of these big old houses."

Everyone got out of the car including Cindy. They walked up to the big front porch with stucco bannisters and rang the bell.

"Is it empty?" Mark asked.

"Who listed this?" Cindy asked.

"Someone lives here. The Pike Valley office listed it. I wonder why they gave it to those bums," John said.

"Let's get in and get out quick," Cindy said.

"There isn't even a lockbox," John said. "What if no one is home, derelict listing asshole?"

"Sh!" Helen said.

An elderly lady opened the door dressed in nice clothes and jewelry wearing makeup. Her hair was done like she just got back from the beauty shop. She smiled and stood back from the door so they could come in.

"Hello," Helen said. "I hope we aren't bothering you."

"Oh, no, I was just waiting on my son to get here," she said. "He said some people from the real estate company would be coming by."

"That would be us. Are you Joey Romeo's mother?" Cindy asked.

"Yes, I am," she said. "Come on in."

"It's nice to meet you. Why are you selling?" Cindy asked.

"I have a house in Florida I may move into. I'm getting too old to make the trip, and the winters here are getting longer it seems to me."

"They sure are," Cindy said. "Is it okay if we just walk through?"

"Of course, be my guests," she said.

"How did you know she was Romeo's mother?" Helen asked as she and Cindy walked into the kitchen.

"I saw her name on a piece of mail in the mailbox by the door. Angela Romeo," she said.

John and Mark walked past them into a family room in a back addition. Helen and Cindy walked upstairs to the bedrooms which were typically on the small side with small closets and one bathroom.

"One thing about mobile homes, at least the closets are bigger than the ones in these old houses," Cindy said. "I guess they had just one nice outfit for church and a moo-moo."

"It's clean," Helen said, "and in great condition. Look at that bedroom suite. I love that vanity. I wonder if she'd sell any of her antiques."

They walked back downstairs where Mark and John were questioning Mrs. Romeo about the age of the roof.

"It's a tile roof. I don't know exactly how old it is, though," she said. "I have trouble remembering my own age."

"Would you sell any of your antiques, Mrs. Romeo?" Cindy asked.

"Which pieces interest you?" she asked.

"The bedroom set with that gorgeous vanity," Helen said.

"I'll have to make up my mind which pieces I want to keep. The vanity appraised for $2,000, just the vanity," she said. "It was handed down to me from Italy."

"We have to be going now, but maybe in a couple days we could come back and look again. We have a lot of houses to see today," Cindy said.

"Thank you for allowing us to see your home, Mrs. Romeo," John said.

"You're welcome," Mrs. Romeo said and followed them back to the front door. "I hope you will come again."

"Thank you," Cindy said.

Walking back to the car Cindy sighed. It's going to be a long day, she thought.

"That sucks that Joey didn't have his mom list with you, Cindy," John said.

"She's an adult. I guess she listed with someone she knew," Cindy said.

"One down and fifteen to go," Helen said.

CHAPTER 8

F rank anticipated a long boring day as he drove slowly off the hill in his Trans Am that morning with the windows rolled down and the radio up with time to spare. His new job at the newspaper was a convenient way to leave his previous position gracefully, but it was not in any way a 'step up'. He wasn't making as much money, and he didn't have a 401K, but he figured he'd let the past stay where it belongs, way back there in the rearview mirror. His divorce after four years of marriage to his college sweetheart was less than amicable, and she wasn't the type to let bygones be bygones. Frank wondered what ever happened to happily ever after.

Clarksville was a coal town where most people were in bed by nine o'clock. The newspaper office was located in an old building in town with free parking across the street. The owner of the paper, Jay Blake, was anxiously watching for Frank and spoke up as soon as he walked in the door.

"We have to get going. There was an explosion at the bank," he said.

Frank at first thought he was kidding but then took note of Jay face, absent of color, and his eyes were bugging out.

"Really?" Frank asked.

"Let's go," Jay said.

Frank turned around and walked back out the door following Jay. Frank had his camera, and Jay was carrying his photo ID in his hand. The sirens of fire trucks and ambulances suddenly filled the air.

"Do you mean like dynamite?" Frank asked.

"I don't know, it just happened," Jay said. "You must've come down North Street otherwise you'd have run right into it."

"Yes, I did. I got a room at the bed and breakfast."

People were running and standing around the bank. Several cars were parked in front and all around the bank, lights flashing and traffic blocked behind barriers being diverted away from the area. One guy was walking back up toward Jay and Frank.

"Why? What happened?" Jay asked him.

"A bomb went off in Cecil Pratt's office. The FBI is there."

"Thanks," Jay said, and he and Frank picked up the pace to a run.

"How could the FBI already be there if it just happened? Even by helicopter, I don't see how," Frank said.

"Maybe they were in route to somewhere else and got the word to come here," Jay said. "Or maybe they caught a ride with aliens."

"You don't have to be a smartass," Frank said, and Jay laughed.

As they approached the crowded area, Jay showed his press ID as they walked around a barrier.

"We're with the Chronicle. Let us pass, please."

The bank employees were standing in a row, waiting to be interviewed one by one. The door from one of the offices had been blown out, and splintered boards and debris were scattered on the charred carpet. Frank snapped a photo. Jay walked over to the employees and a couple policemen.

"Does anyone know anything?" Jay asked.

"A package exploded in Cecil's office. The FBI is in there. An ambulance took Cecil," one of the tellers, Ruby, answered.

"Do you know which hospital they were taking him to?"

"General."

"What was his condition?" Jay asked.

"Not good. He was bloody and burned. His clothes were torn clear off him. I wish we could go home. That made me sick, but I don't think they're going to let us. It doesn't look like it, anyway," she said.

"Did the package come in the mail or what?" Jay asked.

"That's what we have to find out," one of the police investigators said.

"Was it a robbery?" Jay asked.

"Doesn't look like it," the policeman said. "I'm surprised you guys got in."

Jay and Frank looked at one another and shrugged.

"We have business here, too," Jay said. "I recognize you, Sergeant Miller."

"I don't doubt it. I've been a State policeman for twenty years," he said.

"I'm Jay Blake, and this here is Frank Martin. This is Frank's first day at the Chronicle."

Miller stared at him like he recognized him from a wanted poster.

"Hello," Frank said. "It's nice to meet you even under such horrible circumstances. How did the FBI get here so fast?"

"I asked them that," he said.

"What did they say?" Frank asked.

"It's none of your damned business. That's what they said."

It was late when Cindy got back from chauffeuring everyone to see all the new real estate listings. She didn't see Blossom's car parked in her usual spot. When she got back home she saw that Blossom's car wasn't in her driveway either. The red painted dirty word was painted over so that you couldn't even tell it now. Jason was doing his homework when she walked inside.

"Hi, Sweetie. Did you see Blossom today?" she asked Jason.

"No," he said. "Why?"

"I'm supposed to clean for her today."

Cindy got a couple cans of soup out of the cabinet and a box of crackers.

"I'll make us some tomato soup and grilled cheese. Okay?"

"Yep. What is this word, Mom? T-H-E-O-R-Y," he spelled out the letters.

"Theory," she pronounced. "It's a speculative idea based on belief rather than concrete evidence. I have a theory that if we eat this soup and sandwich, we'll have enough energy to clean Blossom's trailer."

"Ah, Mom. I want to go to the gym and play basketball," he said.

"Okay. I'll take you to the gym after you finish your homework and after we eat, then I'll pick you back up after I finish cleaning for Blossom. Deal?"

"It's a deal, Mom," he said.

After they ate she took Jason to the gym at their school which was left open for the students during the evening until seven-thirty. It was a separate building from the school.

"I'll be back by seven-thirty, that's an hour and thirty minutes," she said. "Don't leave with anyone and stay inside until I come in and get you."

"Okay. Thanks, Mom," he said and got out of the car and walked into the gym.

She went back home and looked over at Blossom's trailer. Her car still wasn't there. She parked and walked to Blossom's and lifted up the mat and found the key and let herself in to clean. She saw dirty dishes in the sink and on the table and started clearing off the table. She picked up a card off the table. It was red, white and blue with a round coffee cup stain on it. It was Jack Higgins' Medicare card. She set it on the middle of the table under the napkin holder and washed the dishes and wiped the counters. She found the broom and mop in the corner and swept and mopped the kitchen floor.

She found the vacuum cleaner in the coat closet and vacuumed the living room. She dusted the coffee table and picked up magazines and emptied ashtrays. She started up the hallway vacuuming, then stopped and took some clothes off the washing machine and sorted through them and put a load inside to wash. The dryer was empty. She went into the bathroom and picked up the dirty towels and put them into the washing machine.

She opened up the cabinet and found washing powder and a can of Comet. She then scrubbed the basin and bathtub and the tile up around the shower. She pulled the vacuum cleaner up the hallway and into the bedroom looking for an electrical outlet. She was startled to see Blossom lying on the bed.

"Blossom," she said. "Are you asleep?"

Blossom didn't respond. Cindy thought she may have been crying after what happened and glanced at her watch. It was seven o'clock. She didn't want to wake her and set the vacuum aside. She quietly let herself out and went back to the gym to pick up Jason.

CHAPTER 10

Tuesday was Nikki's first day on her new job at the beauty shop, and she couldn't have been more pleased. The shop looked even better than she imagined with new appliances and a jazzy purple and black motif. She called the newspaper and placed an ad, and then asked if Frank was there.

"Frank," Shirley said. "It's for you."

Frank picked up the phone and answered.

"Frank here," he said. "Can I help you?"

"Would you like to take a spin in my electric chair?" Nikki asked softly.

Frank didn't know who it was until she started laughing.

"Nikki," he said. "I guess I should plead the fifth."

"I'm just trying to drum up a little business here at the shop, and you need a haircut, so come on over after work."

"Okay. I can do that."

"I bet you didn't count on such an exciting new job. What do you think happened? Do they know anything?" she asked.

"Nothing much. I think someone was trying to rob the bank, and that was supposed to be a diversion, but of course that's just a theory. The FBI was there immediately. Maybe they got a tip. They can't say they were looking for weed this time of year," he said. "Where is your shop?" he asked.

"I'm at the truck-stop, in the back where the laundry room is and the pinball machines," she said. "Go through town on Main Street and make a left at the Y, go a couple miles until you see the truck-stop on the left. I'm sure you've noticed all those semis parked there. Come around to the back of the building, and I'm the first door on the right."

"Okay, I'll be there as soon as I get off work."

Shirley watched Frank, and when he hung up she asked him how he knew Nikki. He said he'd just met her. Shirley was crippled with arthritis, but she refused to quit working. She had been there for thirty-five years, longer than anyone else. Jay was the original owner's son, not the man his daddy was, she thought, but he was alright.

"I've known Nikki since she was a little thing. She still is for that matter" Shirley said. "I have to call her back and get an appointment myself. She wants this ad put in the paper for her shop."

"I'm going to go back over to the bank. Where is Jay this morning?"

"He's at a meeting with the Funeral Director about their advertisement. He said he'd be back around ten, though."

"The deadline for ads is two o'clock on Tuesdays, in case you weren't told."

"I'll keep that in mind," Frank said. "I shouldn't be long."

Frank walked to the bank enjoyed the springtime fresh air and sunshine. Clarksville was mostly rural not as populated as Peterstown, but there was a liveliness about it that seemed to have left Peterstown. Frank walked into the bank and noticed the FBI agents were there talking to the president of the bank.

It looked as if their meeting was about to end as they walked a few steps toward the door at a time. The clean-up had been done, and an insurance adjuster was there accessing the damage. Frank waited until they left then approached the bank president, Mr. Hamrick.

"Hello, Mr. Hamrick. I was hoping to ask you a couple questions about the explosion. I'm with the Chronicle, Frank Martin," he said. "Do you have a couple minutes?"

"Just a couple," Mr. Hamrick said. "Come on in to my office."

Frank followed him to his office on the other side of the lobby, and they sat down at his desk. There was a candy dish on his desk filled with sugar candy, and Frank took one and put it in his mouth.

"How can I help you, Frank?" he asked.

"I was wondering how the FBI got here so fast. Do you have any information?"

"I asked them that as a matter of fact, and that young fellow with the thick glasses said he wasn't at liberty to discuss that."

"I thought they may have had a tip that something was about to happen, such as a bank robbery. Do you have any ideas about that?"

"Not really, but we were asked not to discuss anything. Cecil apparently brought a package inside his office which exploded. We don't even know that for sure. Someone could have broken in and planted the explosives the night before. We just don't know."

"Is Cecil going to be alright?"

"I doubt it. He will never be the same after that. We're looking into recent loan applications and foreclosures. That's about all I can say."

Frank stood to leave and reached out his hand to Mr. Hamrick.

"Thanks, Mr. Hamrick," he said and shook his hand and started walking out of his office.

"I haven't seen you around here before," Mr. Hamrick said and followed him to the door.

"Yesterday was my first day at the Chronicle, a little more excitement than what I'm used to. Thank you for your honesty, Mr. Hamrick. I really appreciate it. I won't take up any more of your time. Have a good day."

"Where did you work before, Frank?" he asked as they proceeded down the hallway.

"Peterstown. I worked for the Register previously. I got a room at the bed and breakfast until I find a place. Have you lived here your whole life?"

"Yes, just about, besides the Army for a while, Korea."

"Thank you for your service. I was in Viet Nam," Frank said.

"Take care," Mr. Hamrick said and patted him on the back and left him standing in the lobby.

Frank saw one of the tellers wasn't busy and walked to her window and asked if he could open a checking account and took out some cash from his wallet.

CHAPTER 11

Cindy was at her doctor's appointment feeling anxious and a little upset. She had rehearsed what she was going to say on the way over, but it still sounded stupid.

"I've been seeing things, hallucinating, I guess. I mean certain things will come sharply into focus like a lightbulb went off, but it isn't really that way. One of the guys at my office, for example, I've noticed he is looking, I hate to say this, like a rat. I know that sounds crazy," she said. "A few days ago I was driving through Clarksville, and I saw a homeless man on the street. He looked terrible, but it was a guy I know who isn't even poor, and he doesn't even live in Clarksville. Why would I be seeing things like that?"

"Have you been using drugs?" the doctor asked.

"I have a prescription to help me sleep, but I haven't even been taking them."

"Have you been sleeping alright? Are you under stress?" he asked.

"I've been sleeping better, but I have been under stress recently. My boyfriend has been indicted for racketeering. I didn't know it beforehand, and I really like him."

The doctor started writing her a prescription.

"Two a day with food and water," he said.

"Am I going crazy?" she asked.

"I would break up with that guy, and find someone who isn't going to be spending time in orange jumpsuits."

Cindy's expression was sad and worried. The doctor understood what she must be going through. He opened a cabinet drawer and took out a card and looked at it.

"I'm referring you to a psychiatrist. Dr. Jones. Here's his information," he said and handed her a card. "Make an appointment right away."

"Okay," Cindy said. "Thank you, Doctor Toler."

Cindy drove back to her office and went inside careful not to look over in Bob's direction. She could see there were people in Bob's office, but she was careful not to look. John and Helen were on the phone, and Mark was reviewing what looked like a contract. Cindy sat down and called Romeo first, but he didn't answer. She left him a message to call her.

"Did you make a sale, Mark?" she asked.

"Yes, I sold Mrs. Romeo's house."

"Great! What did it go for?"

"One hundred and ninety thousand," he said.

"That was almost full price, wasn't it?"

"It was listed at $200,000, but it needs some electrical work," Mark said.

"Congratulations, Mark," she said. "If anyone calls, I'll be right back."

Cindy walked to Blossom's office quickly to check on her, but it wasn't Blossom sitting there, it was Mrs. Higgins.

"May I help you, Dear?" Mrs. Higgins said to Cindy.

"I was looking for Blossom," she said.

"Blossom no longer works here," Mrs. Higgins said.

"Oh, my mistake," Cindy said. "I didn't know."

Mrs. Higgins looked back down at her paperwork then reached for the phone and made a call.

"Jack, did you tell me that Cindy is the blond girl that works for Jackson and Greene and is dating Chuck?"

"I may have," Jack said annoyed she had interrupted him while he and Chuck were busy. "Why?"

"She was asking about Blossom. I don't think she knew Blossom had been fired. I thought you said they were good friends."

"I don't know. What the fuck, Boo. Why are you calling?"

"I just wondered if they're such good friends, why she didn't know Blossom was fired."

"Okay, Sherlock. Good luck with the case," he said and slammed the phone down.

Mrs. Higgins giggled and hung up. She enjoyed pushing Jack's buttons. She had an appointment at the beauty shop. She got up and left and locked the office door behind her. When she arrived for her appointment Helen was there, also. Mrs. Higgins couldn't resist bringing up the fact that she fired Blossom.

"I had to fire Blossom. She had her fingers where they weren't supposed to be. I hope she wasn't a friend of yours," Booboo said.

"No, I don't know her," Helen said. "Was there money missing?"

"Not exactly."

"She and one of the other agents live in the same trailer park. Cindy," Helen said.

"I've heard about her. She was looking for Blossom earlier. I know which one she is. She's been seeing Chuck Floyd. Which trailer park do they live in?" she asked.

"At the Golden Years trailer park," Helen answered.

Helen noticed Booboo's ring and thought it had a design on it and asked.

"What's that on your ring? Your wedding date?" she asked.

Booboo looked down turned the ring around.

"No. I dropped it and scuffed it up, I'm afraid," she said.

"Oh. I thought it was an engraving of some kind," Helen said.

CHAPTER 12

J ay was back at the newspaper office by the time Frank returned from the bank. Frank walked over to his desk and sat down.

"Did you have any luck?" Jay asked.

"Not really, but I had to open a bank account anyway. I talked to Mr. Hamrick. He doesn't know much or at least isn't saying much about it. Do you want to go the hospital and see if we can talk to Cecil?"

"May as well. Visiting hours are at two. Let's have lunch at the hospital. They have a good cafeteria," Jay said.

It was about an hour drive to General Medical Center, the closest hospital with a trauma and burn center. Jay knew the local gossip, but he didn't think he wanted to tell Frank about it. Someone without a history in the community like Frank may be more objective without hearing all the gossip. It wasn't anything Jay would write about anyway. His paper may not have a big name with thousands of readers, but it wasn't a rag, either. Instead they talked about Jay possibly running for sheriff the next election. The town's sheriff was elderly and wasn't running for reelection, and Jay could see where it may have its perks for a newspaper reporter. They parked and walked briskly into the hospital and stopped at the front desk.

"What room is Cecil Pratt in?" Jay asked.

"He's in Room 110," the nurse said.

"We're with the newspaper. Can we see him?" Jay asked.

"Not until visiting hours at two," the nurse said.

They had lunch in the cafeteria then walked to the waiting room. There were other people waiting, too, each with their own heartbreak. Their expressions all looked the same as they glanced up at Jay and Frank as if to in sympathy knowing they were all slung together like a train wreck.

"Are any of you here to visit Cecil Pratt?" Frank asked them.

A lady with silver hair and penetrating blue eyes spoke up.

"I am," she said. "I'm his wife. The doctors are in there right now."

"I'm really sorry about what happened, Mrs. Pratt. We're with the newspaper. I'm Jay Blake, and he's Frank Martin. We were hoping to get to speak with Cecil. Do you know who gave him the package or anything about that?"

"He hasn't talked to anyone so far. The doctor said he might even have amnesia," she said. "He seems to be doing a little better."

"That's a blessing," Jay said.

"It's a miracle he didn't get killed," Frank said.

Tears came to Mrs. Pratt's eyes, and she dabbed them away with a tissue.

"Could he have taken the package from home?" Frank asked.

"No," she protested. "There wasn't anything in it except the explosives. They said it had some kind of trigger, not a timer. That's all the FBI would tell me."

"Did the FBI search your house?" Jay asked.

"Oh, yes, they certainly did, with a fine-tooth comb," she said. "They didn't find anything. I knew they wouldn't. Cecil wouldn't know how to make a bomb even if he wanted to, for crying out loud."

"Do you know who could have done it?" Jay asked.

"I have no idea," she said.

"Do you mind if we talk to him, Mrs. Pratt?" Jay asked.

"I don't think it'll do you any good, but you can try if you want."

"It's two now," Frank said. "I guess we could see if they'll let us in."

"Thank you, Mrs. Pratt," Jay said. "We're just doing our job."

"I understand," she said. "You go on ahead."

The others in the room heard what she was saying even though she spoke softly.

Most of them hadn't heard anything about it, and an older man whose daughter had just been in a car wreck asked.

"I hadn't heard anything about a bomb going off anywhere. Where did that happen?"

"At Union Bank in Clarksville," she said.

"Was someone robbing the bank?" he asked.

"Not that they can determine. It appears to have been vandalism, probably someone wanting revenge."

Frank and Jay entered the private room together. Two doctors stood inside his room with their arms crossed.

"Has he spoken to anyone yet?" Frank asked.

"No," one of the doctors said.

Cecil was on a respirator and covered in bandages on his arms, hands, and face and head. There were openings for his eyes and a slit for his mouth, and an IV tube was connected to his arm. They slowly approached his bedside and Jay spoke to him.

"Hello, Cecil. This is Jay Blake from the Chronicle. You sure got yourself into a fine mess," he said. "I was hoping to ask you about the package that exploded. Do you remember the explosion?"

Cecil didn't respond.

"He is conscious, but it's doubtful he remembers anything," the doctor said.

"How long will he be in the hospital?" Jay asked.

"It depends. If he survives, he may require reconstructive surgery."

"Cecil, I hope you have a speedy recovery," Jay said.

They could hear some people talking and walking toward the door. It was Mrs. Pratt and the two guys from the FBI they saw at the bank. They looked at Frank and Jay disapprovingly.

"Has he said anything?" one of the agents asked the doctors.

"No. We may have to put him into a coma. He's in a lot of pain," the doctor said.

Frank and Jay walked back out into the hallway. "We're not going to find out anything from those two," Jay said. "Let's get back to the office."

The drive back to Clarksville seemed longer to Frank. It was almost five when they got back to the office. He hoped Jay didn't expect him to work that evening.

"I have a haircut scheduled," Frank said. "I think I need one."

"Did you see the way those FBI guys looked at us? Like we were turds in a punchbowl," Jay said.

"I'd rather be turds in a punchbowl than jackoffs at a piss parade," Frank said.

CHAPTER 13

Frank drove to the truck-stop with no problem and walked into Nikki's shop. She was sweeping up some hair off the floor and emptied it into a trashcan. Frank stood over six feet tall, almost a foot taller than Nikki. He smiled at her and put his hands over his ears.

"Hear no evil," he said.

Nikki twirled the chair around for him.

"Have a seat."

He sat down, and she draped a cape over his shoulders and leaned the seat back to wash his hair.

"You have great hair," she said.

"Thanks," he said. "So do you."

She washed and towel dried his hair and tossed the towel into the hamper. Frank watched her in the mirror as she combed his hair. He noticed she had hair clips attached all over her purple apron.

"You remind me of Edward Scissorhands, much prettier, though."

"You haven't seen me in the morning," she said holding the scissors over his head like a claw.

"I just remembered I have another engagement," he said and pretended to start to get up from the chair.

She held his shoulders down and looked into his eyes in the mirror.

"I'll go easy on you," she said and picked up a lock of his hair and started snipping.

"Just don't scalp me. Leave a little around my ears," Frank said. "What's the name of your shop?"

"The Clip Joint," she said. "I think aprons and hairclips are making a comeback this spring."

"Did Shirley call you back?"

"Yes, she made an appointment."

"Do you know Jay?" Frank asked.

"I know he started working there when his dad died, about a year ago, and he's still wet behind the ears."

"We went to visit Cecil Pratt in the hospital today. He looks like a mummy."

"I heard he was bad. The FBI questioned one of my friends," she said.

"How was your friend involved?"

"His car was parked on the street nearby when the bomb went off. He had stopped to cash a check on his way to work."

"They must think someone handed Cecil the package from outside the bank."

"I guess they have to explore all avenues. I heard that maybe the bomb was meant for someone else, like Cecil was supposed to give it to someone else. Then I heard they said someone may have broken into the bank the night before and just set it down on Cecil's desk."

"I think someone meant to rob the bank," Frank said.

"Cecil?"

"I don't know, maybe."

"I can't see Cecil doing anything like that, and he doesn't have any enemies."

"Everyone has at least one good enemy," Frank said.

Nikki continued to snip off locks of hair that fell onto the floor. Then she held his face straight to look into the mirror.

"Is that short enough for you?" Nikki asked.

"Perfect. I'll have to go get my picture took now," he said.

He stood up to leave and handed her a ten dollar bill. He paused wanting to ask her out.

"Keep that. I told you it's on the house," Nikki said.

"No. Would you like to go out to dinner with me?" he asked.

"I can't. My son is waiting on me to fix his dinner. You can come home with me and join us for dinner, though. We're having macaroni and cheese with brown beans and cornbread."

"Gosh, that sounds good," Frank said. "Really?"

"Yes, really. I'm a pretty good cook. Let me clean up, and you can follow me home," Nikki said.

She started sweeping up Frank's hair.

"My son, Jeremy, has a babysitter across the street. They have two little boys, and they all get along well, but Jeremy won't eat anywhere but at home. He's a picky eater."

"How old is he?"

"He's seven," Nikki said and took off her apron and grabbed her purse. "His dad lives in Princeton, and gets him every other weekend."

"My wife and I didn't have any kids," Frank said. "Where does your friend, Cindy, work?"

"She works for a real estate company in Princeton. She and her son Jason come to her parent's house most weekends. We're like sisters," she said. "Okay, follow me."

CHAPTER 14

Blossom had been waiting at the shop to get her car out of the garage. Fortunately, she had collision coverage with a zero deductible or she really would be up-shit-creek. She hit a deer on the way home as if getting fired wasn't bad enough. The windshield and the side mirror had to be replaced. In a way she was relieved. Now she could divide her misery into two. Jack had done all he could to keep her on without causing a riot. She couldn't blame him. He even gave her cash for severance pay.

She noticed Cindy was home. She hadn't had a chance to thank her for cleaning her trailer. She'd been so upset she had taken a couple sleeping pills and didn't even know Cindy had been there.

She pulled over in front of Cindy's and walked up to the door and knocked. When Cindy saw it was Blossom she opened the door anxiously.

"Hey, Blossom. Come on in," she said.

"Hi, Cindy. I wanted to thank you for cleaning my trailer. It was really a nice thing to do. You don't even know. Thanks."

"You're welcome. I didn't see your car, and I thought you weren't home. I would've cleaned your bedroom, but I didn't want to wake you. Was that alright?"

"That was perfect. I woke up around four in the morning, and saw how clean the place was. I thought, oh, my God, Cindy was here! It made me feel a lot better after getting fired and hitting a deer all in the same day."

"Oh, no. I hate it when that happens. Did it do a lot of damage?"

"The windshield and side mirror had to be replaced. They said I was lucky it didn't come in on me. That was the first one I ever hit. Where's Jason?" she asked.

"He has a sleep-over tonight with one of his classmates. His dad's taking them out for pizza. I stopped by your office, and Mrs. Higgins said you no longer work there."

"Right. She fired me."

"She fired you. What did she say?"

"She came into the office and said 'You need to get your things and leave, NOW'. I just got my stuff and left without saying a word. Jack tried to have me stay on, but she wasn't having it. Did you see what someone did to my trailer?"

"Jack stopped and showed me that morning," Cindy said. "Did he spend the night?"

"No. He came by Sunday evening and gave me severance pay, but he just stayed a few minutes. He came back that morning looking for his Medicare card. He thought he may have dropped it when he was taking money out of his wallet. He left to get paint and a ladder and came right back and painted it himself. I was glad of that. I said if I find out Booboo did that, I'll beat her ass. He said no, she wouldn't have the balls.

"Who else would have done it?" Cindy thought out loud.

"Jack said maybe Susie did it or had someone to do it. I used to work with her in housekeeping. Before I got a promotion I was making beds when her husband from maintenance came in and tripped over some laundry on the floor and fell over top of me when I was making the bed. The guy working with him that day saw it, and he had to go running his mouth. Maybe Susie thought there was something going on between us. No way would I be with that hick, but you know how people are," Blossom explained. "I don't think Susie would do that, though. I've known her a long time, and she always seemed like a good person to me, not the type to stoop to that level. I should have called her and talked to her about Jeff right then, but my grandma always used to say the more you stir shit the worse it stinks, so I kept my mouth shut."

"I saw Jack's Medicare card on your table. It was under some dishes. I put it under the napkin holder."

"Really? We looked everywhere for it and didn't see it. I'll have to mail it to him," Blossom said.

"Do you want to go somewhere for dinner and a drink? I don't go out around here or get the chance to very often," Cindy said.

"Sure," Blossom said. "Let's celebrate. I've never had a month's pay in advance before, in cash! Let's go somewhere with good hors d'oeuvres. I'm hungry."

"I could go for some hors d oeuvres. I had a doctor's appointment and skipped lunch today," Cindy said.

"What's wrong?" Blossom asked.

"I've been seeing things, hallucinations, really weird shit. Doctor Toler gave me a prescription and told me to call a psychiatrist and to stop seeing Chuck. I hate to, but I think if I don't stop seeing Chuck, I'm going to get into trouble, or lose my mind, apparently."

"I know what you mean," Blossom said. "There is no middle ground with those guys. I always liked Jack and even Booboo, but I can't help their luck. You know what I mean?"

"Yep. I know what you mean. It's like we have nothing better to do than pick up their pieces," Cindy said.

They drove a few miles out of town and pulled in at the Rose Café. Several cars were parked along the road on both sides, and Blossom parked at the end of a line of cars on the other side of the road and skipped a car space.

"Hopefully, no one will bang my doors parked here," Blossom said.

They climbed out and walked up to the door and rang the bell looking up at the camera in the corner. The noise buzzed as the latch opened, and they opened the door quickly and walked in to jukebox music. It was a little dark and the tables were all taken except for one in the corner. They sat there while everyone at the bar turned and looked at them. Cindy and Blossom were hungry and decided on pizza. They ordered pizza supreme with a pitcher of beer. Their beer came right away, and each drank before the pizza came. It was really great pizza, and they were eating slice after slice. Blossom asked for a box to take home the leftovers, and she paid the bill, and Cindy left a tip.

"Thanks, Blossom. Here's a ten," Cindy said and stuffed it in her purse. "This place isn't too bad. Good pizza, but I really need to get back."

"Me, too," Blossom said. "I need to find a job."

They drove home listening to music without talking much. Cindy got out and said good night, and Blossom drove on to her trailer.

A few minutes later Cindy heard a knock on her door. She looked out the peephole expecting to see Blossom, but she saw Jack standing there. She was puzzled to see him and wondered if something was wrong and opened the door.

"I need to ask you something," Jack said. "Can I come in a minute?"

Cindy stepped back from the door, and Jack walked in and over to the sofa and sat down without being asked. He set his pistol down on Cindy's glass coffee table making a noise as the metal settled on the glass. Cindy was stunned, too stunned to say anything. She continued to stand and just looked at Jack without speaking.

"Let me just say I respect you, Cindy. I know you work hard, and you're a good mother to your son. I have a proposition for you. It really doesn't require anything of you. You go to Clarksville practically every weekend, right?"

"Yes," Cindy said.

"All I need is a key to the trunk of your car. You won't know anything about it, but I'll have some pot put into your trunk the night before, then when you get to Clarksville I'll have the pot taken out of your trunk when you aren't around. You just park in a safe place, and they'll take out the pot without anyone seeing. You'll be paid a hundred dollars each time. That's enough to make a house payment."

"I can't do that," Cindy said.

"You won't know anything about it," he said.

"You just told me. I can't do that. Do you know how many of my friends have been busted for pot?"

"You won't know anything about it. It's an easy way to make extra cash."

"I know you say that, but you told me, and I don't want to do that. If I would get stopped, or have a wreck, or whatever. No. I can't do that."

"Just think about it."

"No, thank you," Cindy said. "I have a son."

Jack sat looking up at her still standing there.

"Don't mention what I asked you to anyone," he said.

He got up from the sofa and picked up the gun from the table and put it under his belt in back. Cindy backed off into the kitchen as he walked toward the door and opened it. He turned and looked at her standing there like a frightened child and felt a twinge of guilt.

"Good night, Cindy," he said and left.

CHAPTER 15

The FBI agents were hoping Cecil Pratt would recover with his memory, but there was no proverbial light at the end of the tunnel, and the prospect of him making a recovery seemed slim. The group sat together at a round table inside their new offices grasping at straws.

Tom Bandy was the one with the thick black-rimmed glasses. He was in his forties and putting his first kid through college with another right behind him. His grandmother was murdered when she was fifty, and the murderer had gone unpunished due to mishandling of evidence. His coworkers admired him for his work ethic, and his family depended on him and trusted him with their lives. He was the one at the bureau that garnered the most respect among the other agents. He was the head of the round table. He sipped on his coffee as the others waited for his lead. He picked up a piece of paper and looked at it then handed it to Agent Taylor.

"Here is an artist rendering of the person reportedly seen handing Cecil Pratt something prior to going into the bank the morning of the explosion. The witness is basically a bum who spends most of his time sitting in front of the beer joint in town looking for two-dollar hookers. Show it around, Taylor," he said addressing Agent Taylor. "It's all we got."

Taylor took the drawing, looked at it and made no comment. Agent Bandy had an annoyed expression on his face as he continued.

"We don't have a problem with people talking, everyone's very friendly, but no one knows anything. It may have been someone who was turned down for a loan or a foreclosure, or it could be someone with a personal agenda. There is no evidence suggesting a robbery attempt. Even though some of the markings on the window were consistent with a break-in, there is a lot more evidence to show that it was an explosion that blew out the glass from the inside. The doctors say Pratt probably won't remember it even if he recovers. Mrs. Pratt seems very upset… even though she and Mr. Hamrick have been having an affair for years according to the local gossip, anyway. She says they were just friends. Cecil didn't have much life insurance, fifty thousand. We've interviewed everyone who had a foreclosure or repo last year, and everyone turned down for loans, but none of them were in town that morning and can account for their whereabouts, just a lot of dead ends."

Tom waited for comments, but no one said anything.

"What about the Higgins case?" another agent asked. "Have we gotten any evidence against Jack Higgins?"

"Just the one witness, Porter, and his credibility is a big problem. We have listening devices at his office and inside his house, but Jack Higgins is about as closed-mouthed as Cecil Pratt."

"What about those girls, Blossom and Cindy? What do we know about them?"

"They're party girls. I think Nikki Detrapano is the one to watch. She was seeing that jerk, George Barker, and we know he and Porter were in bed together. Now she's keeping company with that reporter we saw at the bank, Frank Martin."

"Should we put a tail on her?"

"No. We have a listening device inside her shop. Check out Higgins Hotel guest book for February. Without the testimony of Porter, we don't have a case against Higgins unless we can turn up something else. Porter is saying now that he had Higgins mixed up with someone else, Sam Freeman, and now he's recanting his previous statement."

Porter was a small fish compared to Higgins by FBI estimation, and their disappointment was profound.

"How could anyone confuse Sam with that ugly old bastard? Tell me that," Taylor said.

"Sam is no prima donna," Tom said.

"I could check out that reporter, Frank Martin. He worked at the Register in Peterstown prior to moving to Clarksville. I could check that out," Jenkins said.

"Okay, do that. You can go ahead," Tom said.

CHAPTER 16

Agent Jenkins stopped at the corner of Sycamore Street on Route 19 and parked beside the historical marker. It was the home of the largest alluvial diamond ever found in North America discovered in 1928 when the Jones family found it in their own backyard while pitching horseshoes. Jenkins had heard the story before. The Jones family lived through the depression not realizing it was a diamond and worth a fortune. Jenkins thought how strange that West Virginia, a state best known for its coal production, would, also, be the home of North America's largest, 34.8 carat, diamond, until 1984 anyway when it was auctioned off to an Asian country.

It was eleven o'clock, and Jenkins rolled down his window and smoked a cigarette before continuing to the newspaper office. When he walked in he was greeted by a pretty young woman chewing gum and talking on the phone. She discreetly excused herself from the call and hung up.

"Hello, how may I help you," she asked.

"Hello. I'm looking for a job as a reporter," Jenkins said. "I heard you may have an opening."

"Yes, as a matter of fact, we do. Do you have experience as a reporter?"

"Yes, I do," he said.

She pulled out a drawer and reached him an application.

"Here's an employment application. You may sit over there and fill it out," she said.

"What happened to the previous reporter?" he asked as he took the application from her hand.

"D-I-V-O-R-C-E," she sang like Tammy Wynette

"I guess he got caught with his hand in the cookie jar," Jenkins said and grinned.

"She got tired of his bad habits."

Jenkins raised his hand to his mouth and tipped his head back to indicate drinking.

She nodded and sighed as if it was the end of civilization as we know it.

"I don't want to take sides, though. My husband and Frank are pretty good friends."

"Who is your husband?"

"My husband is Donnie. He works at the Board of Education where Susie works, Frank's wife, X-wife, works, also," she said correcting herself. "Susie and Frank are good people, but they never did get along. I'm Penny, by the way," she said and turned her name plate around facing him.

"I don't mean to bug you, Penny. I like to know what the story is, though," he said smiling sheepishly. "Can I take this application with me and bring it back? I have an errand to run."

"Sure, no problem," she said and snapped her chewing gum.

Jenkins was kind of cute, Penny thought, with his dark curly hair and blue eyes.

"I'll see you later, Penny," he said. "Thanks."

He went back to his car and drove around the block looking for the Board of Education office. He circled the block and parked in front. He sat in his car a few minutes and smoked another cigarette.

He then walked into the Court House to the Circuit Clerk's office and looked for Frank's divorce information to see if it included a settlement agreement. He stood at the tall counter and pulled the large heavy book to the side and read.

Susie got the house, a Toyota and $25,000 of his 401k plus $500 a month for a period of three years, most likely to cover her car payment, he thought. Frank got a Trans Am, the remainder of his 401k, a dog, and a lot somewhere else. That seemed fairly amicable, Jenkins thought, but he wondered about where the extra lot was located and decided to look that up, also. He jotted down the numbers and headed for the real estate records.

It was an acre lot purchased for $10,000. They may have been planning to build there, Jenkins thought. There wasn't anything unusual, just a normal divorce.

Jenkins walked back to his car and opened his laptop and looked up Susan Martin's photo ID. She was a nice looking woman. He watched as people walked out of the Board of Education building and crossed the street to Debbie's Restaurant for lunch. He spotted Susie right away. She had long straight brown hair and wire-rimmed glasses, petite and bouncy. He didn't see much reason to pursue it, but he didn't like the way Frank looked at them at the bank or at the hospital for that matter. He thought Frank seemed a little hostile and wondered why. He decided he may as well have lunch and flirt with Susie a little, no harm in that. He had to eat anyway.

Jenkins waited a couple minutes then went into the restaurant and waited for a table. He saw Susie and a couple other ladies sitting together, and the waitress was taking their order as they sipped on iced-tea. The waitress then came up to Jenkins.

"Just one, Sir?" she asked him.

"Yes," he said.

She walked a few feet to a small table.

"Is this alright?" she asked.

"Yes, thank you."

He sat down, and she brought him a menu and asked what he'd like to drink.

"Just water, please. What's the special today?" he asked.

"Chicken liver and onions with mashed potatoes and gravy and Greene beans, coleslaw, applesauce, corn or macaroni and cheese," she said. "That comes with a roll and a garden salad."

"I'll have that but hold the gravy, with applesauce, and I want French dressing on my salad," he said. "Thank you."

The waitress walked away, and he fixed his gaze on Susie. He watched and waited for her to acknowledge him. Staring at someone gets their attention unless they are just completely zoned out. It's important to quickly look away, though, as if you were caught just admiring a pretty girl rather than anything creepy. When she looked Jenkins glanced away quickly then very slowly back over at her. She was still looking at him and smiled at him knowingly. He gave her a bashful grin and looked away as if embarrassed and coughed, pleased with himself. FBI training had its merits.

Susie and her coworkers ordered hotdogs and fries, the standard lunch for most people in town, only about half the price of anything else other than the beans or vegetable soup with cornbread which was second to the cheapest lunch item, Jenkins thought. He was a big lunch eater himself and didn't have dinner other than liquor since his wife divorced him after ten years of marriage. It still hurt a little whenever he thought about it. He needed to find someone to take his mind off her, but he hadn't. It had been six years, and he was falling more deeply in love with a bottle of liquor.

His meal came in a few minutes. He finished eating trying to overhear their conversation at Susie's table, but they spoke quietly, and he couldn't distinguish what they were saying. His meal was excellent, though, and he felt immensely satiated.

The ladies got up to leave as he picked up his bill and took some money out of his shirt pocket. He left a two-dollar tip on the table and followed Susie to the register. She paid and turned to smile at him again before leaving, and he smiled back at her politely.

"Hi," he said. "Beautiful day, isn't it?"

"Yes, it is," she said as she waited in line to pay for her lunch.

"I'm site-seeing today," he said.

"Oh, where are you from?" she asked.

"Blacksburg," he said. "And you?"

"I live here in Peterstown. I work for the board of education."

"It's nice to meet you."

"I'm Susie. It's nice to meet you, too. Enjoy your day."

She paid her bill and walked out with the others. Jenkins paid his bill and watched the ladies go back into the yellow-stone building as he walked back to his car and decided to drive back over to the newspaper office.

"I'm sorry, but the boss has left for the day," Penny said when Jenkins walked back into the office. "He said he was sorry he missed you. What did you say your name is?"

"Sparks, Will Sparks," Jenkins said. "I may check back in a couple days. Did you all write about the bank robbery in Clarksville?"

"Yes," she said.

"I'd like to see the article on it if I may," he said. "May I buy a paper, please?"

"Here, you can have it," she said and pointed out the article in the paper.

He read the short article.

"It's hard to imagine someone doing that for no reason," he said.

"There must have been a reason. See, Frank Martin, he wrote the article, and he's the one who left our employment," she said and pointed to his name.

"He wrote the article before he left?"

"No. He's still writing for us pro bono until we can find a replacement, for a couple weeks, anyway."

"Sounds like a spur of the moment decision. I'm not that carefree," Jenkins said.

"We weren't expecting it, if that's what you mean," Penny said. "He kept his plans to himself, but since his divorce, I guess he needed a change of scenery."

"Thanks, Penny," Jenkins said and left.

CHAPTER 17

Agent Taylor drove to the bank in Clarksville with the artist rendering of their suspect and walked into the lobby and asked to speak with Mr. Hamrick. The receptionist rang his desk, and she told Taylor he could go on in. He passed the room which was now under reconstruction and went into Mr. Hamrick's office.

"Hello, Mr. Hamrick," he said.

"Hello," Mr. Hamrick said and stood.

"That noise must drive you up the walls," Taylor said.

"I've used more aspirin in the last week than I have in years. How can I help you?"

"I have the artist rendering here of a suspect seen handing Mr. Pratt something before he came into the bank that morning."

He reached the drawing to Mr. Hamrick. He looked at it and shook his head.

"I have no idea," he said. "I don't see many people on a daily basis like the tellers and loan officers. Did you ask them?"

"I wanted you to see it first," Taylor said.

"I heard Cecil has taken a turn for the worse. I guess we should be thankful we weren't robbed, but whoever did that to Cecil should get the chair."

"I agree. I'll check with the others. Thank you."

"I'd like to see if anyone knows who that could be," Hamrick said and followed Taylor back out into the lobby.

After passing the drawing around everyone just shook their head no except Ruby.

"That kind of looks like Millie McClary, the school cook." she said.

That seemed amusing to the others who chuckled.

"Is that supposed to be the person who gave Cecil the package?" Ruby asked.

"The witness may be less than credible," Taylor said. "For which school does she work?"

"She works at the elementary school on Church Street," Ruby said.

"Thanks, everyone, for your time. I appreciate your help," he said and walked away.

Mr. Hamrick stood in the lobby looking out the front window watching as Taylor quickly left the building.

Taylor could get to the school before they closed if he hurried. It didn't seem likely, but he had to follow any leads. He drove there and walked quickly to the doors just minutes before school let out. He walked through the empty hallway to the principal's office. The principal was Mrs. Waters who sat at her desk preoccupied with paperwork. He stood quietly until she looked up at him after a couple minutes.

Her expression was clear, what the hell do you want? But she didn't say a word.

"Hello, Principal Waters. I'm Agent Taylor with the FBI."

Her demeanor changed slightly.

He showed her his ID, and she looked down at it then back up at him without moving her head.

"I need to ask you a question," he said.

He presented the drawing, and she studied it for a moment.

"Does that look like anyone you know?"

"No," she said.

"Someone said it resembled a cook who works here at this school."

"Who?"

"Humor me. Was Mrs. McClary working on the day of March 12th?

"I believe so."

"Can you check and make sure and tell me what time she clocked in?"

"Of course," she said.

She walked to the file cabinet and checked the time cards. She was surprised to see that Mrs. McClary had not worked that day. It was rare that she called in sick. She informed Agent Taylor that Mrs. McClary was not there at all that day.

"She called in sick," she said.

"Thank you," he said.

CHAPTER 18

Agent Taylor then drove to Higgins Hotel. He walked into the lobby around four o'clock and stopped at the front desk. His snappy appearance caught the eye of the concierge whose desk was in the far corner of the lobby.

"I need to speak with the owner," Taylor said to the receptionist at the front desk.

She picked up the phone, and Taylor turned to look at the concierge. Danny's head quickly jerked back. Anyone could see that Taylor wasn't the usual vendor, and Taylor could tell Danny wasn't the usual concierge. He was wearing lipstick and a feather in a purple hat. He looks like Prince, Taylor thought.

The receptionist rang the office of Mrs. Higgins.

"There is a gentleman here to see you," she said.

Agent Taylor took his badge out and flashed it for her to see.

"He's with the FBI," she said in a hushed voice and hung up the phone. "She said she'll be out momentarily. You may have a seat if you'd like."

Taylor walked over and sat on the brown leather sofa. From there he could see through the glass walls into the real estate offices. They look busy, he thought. He figured most of their business was in Pearisburg and Blacksburg, Virginia, just a few miles across the state line. He noticed the cute blond and thought she must be Cindy.

"Hello," Mrs. Higgins said as she stood in front of the sofa a few feet away. "Shall we go into the restaurant for a cup of coffee and talk?"

"That won't be necessary. What I need is your guest book, back to the first of the year," he said as he stood.

"Do you have a search warrant?"

"We are looking for a fugitive who we believe may have been staying here," he said ignoring her question.

Mrs. Higgins contemplated briefly and thought it would be better to go ahead.

"My husband isn't here. If he has no objection, you may. Let me call him and ask."

She picked up the phone on the front desk and called.

"Agent Taylor with the FBI is here. He's asking to see the guest book.

She hung up the phone.

"Give me the guest book," she said to the receptionist, and she handed her a book. "I'll bring it back in a little while. Just use this if you need it."

She picked up a notebook and glanced through it and handed it to the clerk.

"Follow me," she said to Taylor

They left the lobby and went into Mrs. Higgins' office. She handed him the book.

"Is there someone in particular you're looking for?" she asked.

"Is there an alphabetical listing?" he asked.

"No. Go ahead and have a seat," she said and pulled out a chair to the front of her desk then walked back behind her desk and sat down.

"Do you have many foreign guests?" he asked her as he sat across from her leafing through the book.

"Not usually. I was in Florida all winter and just got back a few days ago," she said.

"How many front desk employees do you have?" Taylor asked.

"Four, two full-time and two part-time."

"Who was working on the evening of February 14th?" he asked as he scanned down the pages.

"I'll have to look and see."

She walked over to the file cabinet and pulled out a drawer and leafed through time cards until she found it.

"It looks like Blossom Moses worked that evening, but she no longer works here. I don't know why she would have been working the front desk, though. That wasn't her job. She may have been filling in for someone who called in sick."

"I see. Who did she fill in for?"

"I don't know. I don't have that information right now, and besides that would be against privacy laws."

Taylor noted a name he recognized as an alias who was a guest on February 14th.

Mrs. Higgins saw that Blossom began her position as Human Resource Manager on December 15th.

"Blossom started on December 15th and was let go on March 15th," Mrs. Higgins said.

"That was short and sweet," Taylor quipped.

"She was temporary until I got back from Florida. She lives in a trailer park, Golden Years Park, on 29 Elm it looks like," she said as she read from her file. "Or maybe it's 27."

"So you missed the winter we had. Can you please make me a copy of this page?"

He gave her back the open book and pointed to one of the pages.

"That was the point," she said.

She walked it over to the copy machine and made a copy of the page and handed it to him.

"Your cooperation is appreciated," he said and looked at the page to make sure she'd given him the right page. "Thank you."

"Not a problem," she said.

They walked back to the front desk, and Agent Taylor shook her hand.

"Thanks, again," he said.

"You're welcome. We are law-abiding citizens," she added.

As he turned to leave the concierge couldn't resist winking at Agent Taylor who pretended not to notice and left quickly. Mrs. Higgins gave the book back to the receptionist and watched Taylor get into his car and drive away. She then walked back to her office without comment.

"He was so good-looking, wasn't he?" Danny said to the receptionist.

"You're just horny," she said.

"I liked his haircut," he said. "I wish my hair would do that."

"Whatever."

Mrs. Higgins sat down at her desk and called Jack.

"I gave him a copy of one page on February 14th. He said they're looking for a fugitive and asked about who was working the front desk that evening, and I told him. Blossom," she said.

"Blossom? She wasn't working the front desk," Jack said.

"See for yourself."

"Maybe she was screwing him. That's none of my business," Jack said.

"Okay, Jack," she said and hung up.

He rang her back immediately.

"Don't hang up on me. I want to see that page. Bring it home," he said and hung up.

Booboo had already made a copy of the page and of the time card with Blossom working the front desk and smiled thinking how that would get Jack's goat.

CHAPTER 19

Chuck was there at the gym with Jack when Booboo called and was about to tell Jack something before Boo called. Now Jack was off on another tangent.

"That son-of-a-bitch, Taylor. He damn well knows we didn't have a fugitive staying at the Hotel on Valentine's Day. Boo said Blossom was working the front desk that evening. Maybe someone called in sick or something. She didn't tell me about it. What the hell."

"Did they say who they were looking for?"

"No, but I can check and see who checked in that night. I'll call every damned one of them," Jack said. "I'll say I'm the CIA."

Chuck was quiet waiting until Jack blew off steam.

"I'm not going to prison," Jack said. "They can make up shit a mile long if they want, but no amount of shit is putting me behind bars."

Jack paused and looked at Chuck sitting there like a whipped pup.

"Damn, Chuck, if you need to take some time, I understand. You don't owe me anything."

"I don't want to leave you high and dry," he said.

"You aren't leaving me high and dry. Don't worry about me," Jack said.

"I'm going to take the deal," Chuck said. "The damned Magistrate got busted. He said I sold him cocaine."

"For Christ's sake, when did that happen?"

"I don't know when I was supposed to have sold him cocaine, but Agent Asshole sprang that one on me this morning. He stopped by the grill."

"Have you talked to the Magistrate? What's his name, Phillips?"

"Yes, that's the one, but no, I haven't. I'm tired," Chuck said. "I'm going to take off and go to the beach for a few days. What else can they do to me, anyway, that they haven't already tried?"

"How long do you plan on staying?" Jack asked.

"Not long. I need to tell you something, Jack. I need you to promise me you won't mention this to anyone."

"You know I won't."

"I have an inoperable tumor growing inside my heart cavity. It's a fast growing cancer. The doctors say I have only a couple months to live," Chuck said

"Are you shitting me?" Jack said.

"I wish I was," Chuck said facing downward.

Jack felt a little light headed. Chuck and he went way back. He was practically a son to him.

"I didn't even know you'd been sick," Jack said.

"That's the thing. I haven't been. I mean I cough some, but nothing more than usual."

"Did you get a second opinion?" Jack asked.

"Yes, but it showed up the same. I was wondering if they could have gotten my x-ray mixed up with someone else's. The biopsy came back positive, though."

The sparring match in the ring had turned more ferocious with the sound of leather hitting bare sweaty flesh until one boxer knocked the other one out. He fell hard to the floor and laid there as the other sprang up and down swinging his arms wildly and looked over at Jack and Chuck for recognition, but there wasn't any, and he gradually stopped as if his batteries had died.

"I'll see you when I get back," Chuck said and stood up to leave. "It looks like Johnson is out cold."

Jack jumped into the ring with smelling salts and yelled out, "Get him some water!"

CHAPTER 20

On Saturday morning Chuck phoned Cindy around nine in the morning.

"Hello," Cindy said.

"Are you packed and ready to go?" he asked.

"Yes, but I have to take Jason to my parents first."

"Take your time. I'd rather drive at night. I'll pick you up at your place later tonight, around eleven."

"Okay."

"I'll see you tonight, Baby," Chuck said.

"Okay. See you later. Bye-bye."

Cindy had just gotten out of bed, and Jason was watching cartoons. She made coffee then went in and got a shower. She hadn't been on vacation with a guy before. She and her friends liked going to the beach, and she had picked up her share of guys, but she had never actually been on a vacation with a guy before. Even though this could be the last time she'd ever see him, she was really looking forward to it. It was crazy.

She made scrambled eggs and toast, and she and Jason had a nice breakfast. She was glad there was no hurry.

"Are you ready to go to Mammal's house?" she asked Jason.

"Wait until after this cartoon, Mom," Jason said.

"No hurry."

Cindy decided to call Nikki at her shop.

"This is Nikki," she answered.

"Hello, Nikki. Are you very busy?"

"I'll be working until around three or four. Are you coming up?"

"Yes, but I'm not staying. I'm going to go to the beach with Chuck later tonight. You couldn't work a girl in, could you?"

"What do you need?" she asked.

"Just a trim and wash, just to trim off the split ends," Cindy said.

"Sure. If you can get here around three, I'll work you in," Nikki said.

"I'll be there," Cindy said. "See you later."

Cindy thought she should call Blossom and let her know she'd be out of town and wouldn't be back until the following weekend and dialed her up.

"Hi Blossom. I thought I'd let you know I'm going on vacation. I'll be leaving tonight and probably be gone until next Sunday. Chuck and I are going to the beach, and Jason is staying with my parents. It's Spring break, so this is the ideal time," Cindy said. "I hope I didn't wake you up."

"No, you didn't. I'm going out to lunch with a potential employer," she said.

"Who?" Cindy asked.

"It's a guy I met from Miami. He manages a resort in Miami," she said. "It's a nudist colony."

"Are you kidding?" Cindy asked.

"No. I went to one of their get-togethers last night. They say it's a really nice resort."

"I've never known any nudists before," Cindy said. "What do they do at their get-togethers?"

"Just normal stuff. We played games and had snacks and drinks. It was fun."

"Was it an orgy?"

"Oh, no. It wasn't like that. People just talked and stuff."

"With no clothes on… I can't imagine that. Would I know any of them?" Cindy asked.

"Some of them work for the gas company. Do you know Andi Mack?"

"No," Cindy said.

"Andi's the one who told me about it. I went with her and her husband. She wears wire-rimmed glasses, and one of the guys said she should take off her glasses, and she said no, she needed her glasses. I thought that was funny."

"That would be kind of funny, like what did she need to see? I'll see you next week."

"You guys be safe and have fun. Bye Bye," Blossom said and hung up.

Blossom was feeling a little deserted. It wasn't easy being Blossom.

CHAPTER 21

Blossom liked Cindy, but she was kind of square, she thought. She, on the other hand, was more sophisticated and worldly. She took a shower and put on a little makeup. She was glad she didn't need glasses or contacts. She had 20/20 vision. It was a bit disconcerting seeing people's moles and warts, though, which would typically be hidden from view when clothed. She thought Andi looked good in glasses, and she definitely looked good naked. Most of the others were rather frumpy except for Benny and a couple from Florida looked pretty good naked, she thought as she finished her makeup.

She hurried to the restaurant and stood near the entrance. She was wearing a turquoise wrap dress that really accentuated her curves and showed some cleavage. Booboo was straight as a poker, she thought. She hoped Booboo might notice her there and wonder about the man she was meeting. He was a real catch, not like her wrinkled-up old husband. She might be able to fool Booboo, but not so much herself. She really missed Jack -and working there. She stood nervously waiting until she saw Benny walking toward her and smiled. He was a good looking guy, though… clean-shaven, tall and lean, kind of like a Ken doll.

"Hi, Blossom," he said.

"Hello, Benny."

"I hope you haven't been waiting long."

"I just got here. The waitress hasn't even been over yet."

He got ahold of her arm at the elbow with his arm behind her back and moved in toward her.

"I hope you enjoyed yourself last night," he said.

"I did. I didn't know what to expect, but it was nice. I was pleasantly surprised."

"After the first time you get more comfortable so you won't feel so self-conscious next time," he said.

The waitress showed them to their table, and Benny ordered breakfast.

"I'd like breakfast," he said.

"That sounds good to me, too," Blossom said.

"I like my eggs scrambled, with bacon and a biscuit," he said.

"I'll have the same," Blossom said. "Thank you."

"Coffee?" the waitress asked.

"Orange juice, please," he said.

"I'll have coffee," Blossom said.

Blossom noticed Susie looking over at her and wondered what she was thinking. She probably heard she'd been fired. Susie and she had been pretty good friends. She decided to smile at her and raised her hand and waved at Susie.

"I used to work here," Blossom said.

"Why did you quit?" he asked.

"It was just a temporary position," she said.

Susie walked over to the waitress that waited on Blossom and asked her if she knew the guy Blossom was with, and she shook her head no. Blossom watched from the corner of her eye. Booboo didn't often eat at the restaurant, and Jack was long gone from his usual breakfast time. But of course, word does get around, she thought.

"Who was your boss?" Benny asked.

"Jack Higgins was my boss," she said. "I was Human Resource Manager. His wife was in Florida all winter , and I was filling in."

"I've lived in Florida all my life and graduated from Florida Tech," Benny said."

"How long have you been with the resort?"

"About eight years."

"What is the starting pay, if I may be so bold?" she asked.

"What were you making here?" he asked.

"Not all that much," she said.

"We paid the last girl around $20,000."

"I'm single and have no other income," Blossom said. "I'll have to check out the going wage for your area, and look at the cost of living."

"You won't have rent or utilities to pay, and you'll get your meals at a discount. You won't have to spend all your money on clothes, either. Your pay will go much further, wouldn't you say?"

"Yes, I suppose it would," Blossom said.

"Would you like to have a trial run first?" he asked.

"That would be great," she said.

"I can arrange that," he said. "I'm going to rent a car and drive back to Florida in a couple days. You can ride with me if you'd like. The others are flying back tomorrow, but I have an aunt in Fairmont I'd like to visit before I go back. I haven't seen her in ages. She's my Dad's sister."

"Oh, that would be nice," Blossom said.

The waitress brought their breakfast. As they ate their meal Susie watched curiously. Blossom wondered if the concierge had been fired, also. She could walk back that way and take a look before leaving the hotel. She hadn't expected to find another job so quickly let alone be moving out of state.

"So Blossom, when could you be ready to leave for Florida?" Benny asked.

"I could actually take my own car," she said.

"Oh, no, please ride with me. Then you can fly back. That would be so much easier. You may still have a long drive back to Florida. I hope so, anyway."

"I guess you're right. That does make more sense. Let me think about it. This is a lot to take in."

"I understand. Don't worry, though. You'll be in good hands with me. I promise," Benny said.

They walked out and Blossom waited until Benny left then went back inside the hotel and to the concierge.

"Hello, Danny," Blossom said.

"Hello, Miss Blossom," he said. "How are you?"

"I'm fine," she said. "How is everything with you?"

"So far so good," he said. "I haven't gotten the axe, yet."

"I wondered about that."

"I'm sorry you got fired. Have you found another job?" Danny asked.

"Yes. Actually I just had an interview. It's in Florida, though. I'm a little undecided."

"Which hotel, or is it a hotel?"

"Yes, a resort hotel for nudists," she said.

Danny's expression caused Blossom to laugh out loud. He looked like his eyes were about to bug right out of his head.

"Are you kidding me?" Danny asked.

"No, really. It's a beautiful resort, and people go naked. What could go wrong?"

"Right you are," he said. "I may have to follow you down there. Can you hire me again?"

"Are you willing to get naked?" she joked.

"Oh, I have no problem with that," he said and grinned.

"Oh, my gosh. You'd be perfect! I'll let you know," she teased.

Blossom noticed Danny was wearing lipstick, like Cindy said, but she hadn't really noticed it before.

"I mean seriously," Danny said. "I would love to move to Florida."

"Of course. I'll call you when I get settled," she said.

"It isn't easy working two jobs with no benefits," he said in earnest.

"I understand, and I'll be in touch, Danny."

CHAPTER 22

Cindy arrived for her hair appointment after taking Jason to her parents.

"Wow, Nikki! I love your shop!" she said. "It looks so modern, and purple."

"Isn't it nice?" Nikki said. "I really love it. Have a seat, and I'll get you fixed up."

Nikki put out her closed sign and locked the door. Cindy sat down in the chair and Nikki washed her hair then moved her to the other chair in front of the mirror.

"Do you want about an inch off?" Nikki asked her.

"That sounds about right. Have you been busy all week?"

"I've been averaging four appointments a day so far, not bad. How about you? Are you selling much real estate?"

"Not lately. I thought I'd sell an apartment building to a client of mine, but he's been dragging his feet. I think he needs to get some money together."

"So you are still seeing that guy, Chuck," Nikki said.

"Not for long," Cindy said.

"Why?" Nikki asked.

"He's moving out of state. He's moving to Florida," Cindy fibbed.

"Did he not ask you to move with him?"

"No. This is sort of like a goodbye vacation."

"Gosh, that doesn't sound like much fun," Nikki said.

"I know," Cindy said and laughed. "I need a vacation, though. I'm not going to turn down a free vacation."

"Hey, I don't blame you. Rooms are expensive."

Tom with the FBI was listening intently to their conversation from the bomb squad van parked across the golf course. He drank coffee and sat back in his reclining chair.

"Have you heard anything about the bombing at the bank?" Cindy asked.

"Frank said that Cecil is in a coma now. I don't think they're expecting him to live.

"That's what I heard.

"Are you done for the day now?" Cindy asked.

"Yep."

"Do you have a date with Frank?"

"Yes, I do. How did you guess?"

"You guys make a cute couple."

Nikki held Cindy's head straight then reached her a mirror to look at the back of her hair.

"Is this alright?" Nikki asked.

"That looks much better. Thank you. How much do I owe you?"

"It's five dollars."

"Oh, no it isn't. It is fifteen dollars at least."

Nikki took the cape off her and starting sweeping the floor as Cindy dug out a twenty from her purse and put it down on the counter.

"I hope you have a good time at the beach," Nikki said.

"Me too. Tell Frank I said hello."

"I have time for a hamburger and fries at the lake if you want," Nikki said.

"Okay. Chuck isn't coming until later. He wants to drive at night."

Tom lit up a cigarette and stretched out in the reclining chair. Then he heard Nikki's phone ring. She answered it.

"Hello, Nikki's Clip Joint," she said.

A few seconds passed quietly then he heard her gasp.

"Oh, my God!" Nikki said.

Cindy grabbed Nikki's arm and looked at her wanting her to tell her what was wrong.

Nikki mouthed 'George'.

"He wouldn't have done that. It had to be her," Nikki said.

Nikki shook her head and closed her eyes listening to the details of what must have been a gruesome discovery.

"Ok. I'll talk to you later. Bye," Nikki said and hung up the phone. "Remember George the stalker? He and his wife were found asphyxiated in bed this morning. Someone left the car running with the garage door open into the house."

"Who would have done that?" Cindy asked.

"It had to have been her, not him. He was too full of himself to commit suicide. A neighbor found them."

Tom listened and continued to sip his coffee and smoke a cigarette. So Chuck told Cindy that he was moving to Florida, he thought, unless Cindy was lying to Nikki. Surely, he didn't think he could skip out now.

CHAPTER 23

It was late when Chuck pulled up into Cindy's driveway. She'd been waiting for about an hour wondering if he was going to make it. He blinked his headlights, and she picked up her luggage and pulled the door closed behind her and checked to make sure it was locked.

Chuck got out of the car and offered to help her.

"Can I help you, Sweetie?" he asked.

"I brought only one bag. I'll just put it in the back seat."

"Sorry I'm late. I just kept thinking of things that I needed to do first," he said.

"That's alright."

Cindy got in and snuggled up beside him, and he leaned over and kissed her.

"Where's your luggage?" she asked.

"It's in the trunk."

"I'm a light traveler," she said.

"I would not have guessed that. Your hair looks great. Did you get it cut?"

"Yes my friend Nikki that just opened her shop did it."

"It looks good. Buckle up," he said.

Cindy awoke to daylight when they arrived at the beach.

"Good morning, sleepy-head," Chuck said. "You slept like a rock."

"Good morning. Are we there yet?"

"Yep. Let's take a walk on the beach then we can check into the room. It's still early."

"Okay. Do you have any gum?" she asked.

"Look in the glove compartment. Give me a piece, too."

"Are you tired?" Cindy asked him.

"Not too bad. I'm glad you snore, though. You kept me awake."

Cindy laughed and found the gum and gave him a piece and one for her.

"Sorry about that. I wondered if I snored. Now I know," she said.

"Like a freight train," he said.

"Oh, don't exaggerate," she said.

"I'm not exaggerating. You sound like a chain saw."

Cindy laughed some more.

"I do not. Shut up."

"We can eat at the Waffle House"

"Yes. I like waffles."

"Let's walk on the beach first, then we can have breakfast," Chuck said.

It was a beautiful day with the sun and the sand and the waves washing up over their bare feet. Cindy thought this is the way life should be, or maybe her medicine had finally kicked in. She hadn't been seeing anything strange for a while. She and Chuck held hands and walked, the perfect time to walk on the beach with the sun barely above the horizon, with the sun to their backs.

"I love the way the ocean smells," Cindy said. " Isn't it beautiful?"

Time seemed to stand still, but when the week was up and their fun together was over it was hard to say goodbye. They arrived back at Cindy's early the next Sunday morning. Chuck didn't want to go, and Cindy didn't want him to go, but they didn't really have a choice.

"I don't want you to wait on me while I'm away, Cindy," Chuck said. "You have enough on your plate raising that boy without worrying about me. I mean it."

"I'm so happy we got to do this," Cindy said. "I'm going to miss you."

"I'll miss you, too, more than you know, but I want you to enjoy your freedom, for me. Do you understand? Promise me."

"I promise," she said as tears ran down her cheeks and she turned and got out of the car and walked to her trailer. "She cried for a while then took a shower and washed the sand and Chuck off of her."

CHAPTER 24

Agent Taylor went to the McClary residence and knocked on the door around three in the afternoon. Mrs. McClary came to the door and opened it looking at Taylor standing there with his briefcase in hand and his shiny black car parked in their driveway.

"May I help you?" she asked.

"Yes, maybe you can. I'm Agent Taylor with the FBI. Here is my ID," he said and showed her his ID. "May I come in? I'd like to ask you a couple questions."

She moved back from the door and motioned for him to come in.

"What's this about?" she asked.

She motioned for Taylor to sit on a chair next to the sofa, and she sat on the sofa, then he sat down. The house was clean as a pin, and he could smell dinner cooking.

"I'm just starting dinner. Can I offer you something to drink?" she asked.

"No, thank you. I'll get to the point. I'm sure you heard about the explosion at the bank. A witness said that Mr. Pratt was approached by someone that morning as he was going into the bank. We are trying to establish who that person was who may have spoken with Mr. Pratt that morning. I understand you called in sick that day. Is that right?"

"Well, yes. I had a doctor's appointment that morning. That's where I was going that morning, to my doctor's appointment."

"Were you in town near the bank?"

"No, I wasn't, not at all. I wouldn't take my dog to old Doc Samples," she said of the local physician. "My doctor is in Blacksburg, Virginia. We left around seven-thirty that morning. My appointment was at eight o'clock."

"Was anyone with you?"

"Yes. My friend Clara went with me. Clara Barnett. You can call her and ask her. She's married to Clyde Barnett. They're listed in the book."

"I have an artist rendering of someone who was witnessed that morning speaking with Mr. Pratt just before he went into the bank when the explosion occurred, and some people thought there was a resemblance to you," he said. "I'm sorry to have to bother you, but we have to check out these things whether it makes sense or not."

"I understand, but I can't imagine. Do you have the drawing on you? I'd like to see it."

Agent Taylor opened his briefcase and pulled out the drawing and showed it to her.

"That doesn't look like me," she said. "Do you think I look like that?"

Agent Taylor looked at the drawing and then at her.

"I didn't even see you before today. Are you married?" he asked.

"Is that supposed to be an insult?"

"No. I just meant I didn't know what you looked like until now."

"My husband isn't home yet. He probably stopped by the store. Would you like to stay for dinner?"

"No, thank you. Where does your husband work?"

"He's a coal miner at the Beckwith Mines," she said.

Agent Taylor stood up to leave and Mrs. McClary stood up with him and walked to the door.

"I heard Cecil is in a coma," she said.

"Yes, I believe that's correct," Taylor said.

"It sure is a shame. Cecil didn't deserve that."

"Have you heard anything about who may have been responsible?" he asked.

"No," she said. "I would look at the guys who had their cars repossessed. That's who I would look at."

"Yes, Mam. I think you may be right. What doctor did you see in Blacksburg?"

"Dr. Randal. He's a specialist. I'm diabetic. Can I have that drawing?" she asked. "I'd like to hang it above the fireplace."

"Really?"

"No," she said and shook her head.

"Sorry to have bothered you, Mam. Have a good evening," Taylor said.

Agent Taylor walked back to his car and drove to the edge of town. There was an asphalt plant off the main road which was no longer in operation where he was to meet Agent Jenkins. He pulled into the vacant yard and stopped. The tower stood a couple hundred feet into the air. Taylor saw deer standing at the edge of the woods eating the tall grass. They stood quietly and fixed their gaze upon him. He turned off the car and rolled down his window and lit a cigarette. The deer scattered and jumped into the woods. It was very quiet and peaceful there along the river as he smoked his cigarette. In a few minutes he saw Jenkins' car approaching which pulled up near him and parked. Jenkins got out of his car and walked over to Taylor's open window. Then another black shiny car pulled up behind Jenkins and parked. It was Tom.

Taylor got out of his car and stretched his legs standing beside of Jenkins then Tom walked over to them.

"Did you see the deer standing over there?" Taylor asked.

"Nope," Tom said.

"There were six deer standing there when I pulled up," Taylor said.

"Cecil Pratt died this afternoon," Tom said.

"I'm pretty sure I know who didn't kill Cecil Pratt," Taylor said. "Mrs. McClary was at a doctor's appointment."

"Has that been verified?" Tom asked.

"No, but I'll do that first thing in the morning," Jenkins said. "Her appointment was in Blacksburg with a Doctor Randal."

"The charges against Jack Higgins were dropped," Tom said.

"I knew it. He's as slippery as owl shit," Taylor said.

It was quiet again. They'd been chasing rainbows. Then suddenly a rock was thrown and hit the side of Jenkins' car with a loud thud. They quickly ran to the other side of Taylor's vehicle and hunkered down looking to see where the rock came from. Hidden from sight a row of coal miners were stretched out on the riverbank.

"What the hell! Who's out there?" Tom yelled out.

The coal miners snickered quietly. They were all black with coal dust lying on the muddy river bank peering out over a weedy embankment. Tom took his pistol out of his holster.

"I should come over there and shoot your asses," he yelled. "But I don't want to waste good ammo."

No one made a sound.

"It's probably just some kids," Tom said. "Let's get the hell out of here. I'll see you back at the office in the morning."

Taylor opened his car door and got inside while Bandy and Jenkins ran to their cars and everyone spun out slinging gravel.

The coal miners waited until the coast was clear then walked back down the dirt road along the river bank and stopped at the mom and pop grocery store for a soda. An old screen door slammed shut to the front porch where they sat in old hard-backed chairs and traded fishing stories and other interests such as guns. The school bus stopped there, to let the kids off the bus. The school kids were thrilled to see the coal miners there. They played their usual game of guessing which one of the coal miners may actually be black rather than just a crusty old coal miner. One boy came up to one of the miners they suspected of really being black and asked him that age-old question.

"Is your ass black, too?"

If no one was around, sometimes the coal miner would pull his pants down in the back and say something smart like 'it's just like looking into a mirror isn't it', but today the coal miners weren't in a playful mood.

"I'm going to beat your puny ass if you ever ask me that again," the miner said angrily.

The boys ran back up the dirt road and yelled back at him.

"You're just an old dumbass."

"You better run, you little heathens," he yelled back.

When Mr. McClary got back home he took off his boots and left them on the porch. His wife met him at the door.

"The FBI was here a while ago asking questions about where I was the morning the bank got bombed. I guess I'm one of America's Most Wanted," she said.

"What did you tell them?" he asked.

"I said that I had a doctor's appointment in Blacksburg that morning, and I was nowhere near the bank. He had some drawing he showed me where someone had drawn of a person who was apparently seen talking to Cecil just before he went into the bank that morning. I don't know why anyone would say it looked like me. It didn't look anything like me," she said.

"Cecil died," he said.

"When?" she asked.

"About two o'clock this afternoon.."

"I'll have to take a tray over to Shelby," she said, "and maybe a can of coffee."

"What's for dinner?"

"Meatloaf and mashed potatoes."

"I figured you'd invite the FBI to dinner," he said.

"I did. How in the world do you get so dirty? That isn't even coal. What is that?" she asked looking at him.

"It's mud. We were frog gigging."

"Don't get that on the carpet. Hurry and get a shower before dinner gets cold," she said.

CHAPTER 25

People walked at a snail's pace into the funeral home past the closed casket to briefly hold the hand of Shelby Pratt and offer condolences to the family then popping out the other side of the building. The line started a couple blocks away, but it was a warm sunny day, and people were happy to spend the time exchanging memories with others they seldom saw except for rare occasions such as funerals. Jay and Frank walked from the newspaper office and were finally standing there with Cecil's family, his sons and daughters-in-law and grandchildren.

"I'm sorry for your loss," Jay said. "Cecil will be missed."

"He's in a better place. He isn't suffering anymore," Mrs. Pratt said.

"That's right," Jay said holding her hand briefly.

"Sorry," Frank said.

They passed the closed casket covered in flowers and made their way past the coffee room and back out into the sunshine where the birds sang cheerfully. They walked leisurely back to the office.

"I think it would be a good day to put up some signs. Do you want to go with me?" Jay asked.

"How long will it take?" Frank asked.

"I don't know. Maybe a couple hours," Jay said. "We'll go to areas near the schools where people vote, anywhere there would be good visibility."

"Okay"

"Did you see Nikki?" Jay asked.

"No. Was she there?"

"She was inside the coffee room, I noticed her as we were walking out," Jay said.

"I heard that those FBI guys were back in town. Some guys saw them down there at the old rock quarry," Frank said.

"Really."

"Some guy told Nikki that."

"Who?"

"Brad. She said he told her some coal miners hid on the river bank and watched those FBI guys get out of their cars and were standing together talking, and he got a rock and hit one of their cars."

"Bullshit. What happened?"

"They got back in their cars and took off. Nikki said Millie McClary told her that Agent Jenkins came by her house and asked her some questions about where she was that morning. She said they had a drawing someone said they saw that morning. She had a doctor's appointment in Blacksburg so she wasn't anywhere near the bank, she said."

"Probably Brad Ramsey. He's the only Brad I know, and he works at the mines."

"Nikki said that Cecil's wife and Mr. Hamrick have been having an affair for a long time."

"Everyone knew that," Jay said. "I think he may have killed himself just to make them feel bad. I wonder who made the bomb, though. I don't know why they would suspect Mrs. McClary. What motive would she have?"

"Maybe she just woke up that morning and thought, I'm going to blow Cecil's nuts off. Probably a coal miner who handles explosives, or someone who works on the highways. Are you hungry? I didn't have lunch," Frank asked.

"I could eat. Let's stop and get hotdogs."

"Sounds good. Did you hear about that couple that died from carbon monoxide poisoning?"

"No."

"Some guy named George Barker. His wife left the car running in the garage and left the door open into the house before they went to bed. He was going to leave her. Nikki said he stalked her when she was in beauty-school, and that the FBI called her and told her in was in the mafia."

"I hadn't heard anything about it. We need to start hanging out at the beauty shop more," Jay said.

They went through the drive-thru and got hotdogs and drinks for the road.

"How many signs do you have back there?" Frank asked. "I can hear them rattling."

"A couple dozen."

CHAPTER 26

It was business as usual back at Higgins Hotel. Cindy came in bright and early that Monday morning. It was property inspection day again, and, also, she was supposed to pick up Blossom at the airport that evening. The office was buzzing when she walked in tanned and relaxed. Everyone stopped for a moment, and Dottie spoke to her.

"Hello, Cindy. You sure look nice and relaxed. The beach agrees with you."

"Thank you, Dottie. I feel like the weight of the world was lifted off my shoulders. I really needed a vacation. Who is driving today?" she asked.

"Me," John said. "We have five new listings. One is way out on Watson Ridge, though. Ready?"

"Ready as I'll ever be," Mark said.

"Yes, I'm ready," Cindy said. "Hello, Helen, how are you today?"

"Don't even ask."

"What?" Cindy asked.

"I got called for jury duty," she said.

"Oh, no," Cindy said.

"You might be hearing Jack Higgins and Chuckie," John said.

"No," Helen said. "They dropped the charges on Jack, anyway, and I think Chuck took a plea bargain, didn't he, Cindy?"

"Yes," she said.

"Is he in jail?" John asked.

"I don't know. We didn't talk about it. We had a pact. It was a vacation from reality."

"I don't blame you," Irene said putting on a fresh coat of lipstick. "I would like one of those myself."

"Well, Pilgrims, come along," John said.

They all walked out of the office together, and the concierge spoke to Cindy as they walked through the lobby.

"Hello, Cindy. It's nice to see you back," Danny said.

"Thanks, Danny."

CHAPTER 27

Jack was in the office that morning and was talking with Booboo.

"I told you they didn't have anything on me. You don't listen."

"Don't let it happen again, Jack," she said.

"If you want to worry about something, worry about the damn electric bill," he said.

"I paid it. Unless you want to switch to an alternate power, I don't see much use in complaining about the electric bill. We could put up a windmill or solar panels," she suggested.

"Look into it. I'm going to the gym. Call me if you need anything," he said.

"Have you talked to Chuck?"

"He's at South Central. He'll be there for a while then they'll send him to one of those dormitories for non-violent criminals."

"I'm having roast beef for dinner, your favorite," she said. "Okay?"

"Okay. I'll see you this evening," Jack said.

Mrs. Higgins waited until Jack left then walked through the building and into the restaurant. She was impeccably dressed in a navy blue skirt and jacket with a white and navy Swiss-dot button up blouse and pearls and high-heeled shoes. Her diamond was about as big as her knuckle when she reached up to brush the hair from her face that had fallen over one eye. Men glanced over at her carefully, and women stared at her as she walked up to the counter and sat down for a cup of coffee.

"Good morning, Mrs. Higgins," Susie said. "Would you like a cup of coffee?"

"Yes, please."

Susie poured her a cup of coffee.

"Anything else I can get you?"

"No, thank you. How are you, Susie?"

"I'm fine. Thanks for asking. Did you have a nice time in Florida?"

"Oh, yes. I enjoy seeing my granddaughter and my parents. Dad turned eighty-three in January. My little granddaughter is so precious."

"I heard the charges against Mr. Higgins were dropped. That's good news," Susie said somewhat fearful that she may be offended, but still she wanted to get it out of the way.

"Yes. He told me all along he hadn't done anything, but I told him he can't hang around with people like Chuck Floyd, or he's guilty by association."

"True. How old is your granddaughter?" Susie asked.

"Britt is ten. My Nicki is a good mother, and her husband is a good man. They'll go far, I think."

Susie noticed her apricot lipstick.

"That's a lovely shade of lipstick on you," she said.

"Thank you, Susie. How is Jeff doing?"

"He's doing well. I should thank you for firing Blossom. I'm not so sure anything was going on between them, but anyway. Do you like the real estate company and the new concierge?"

"Not so much. The real estate company has a year-to-year lease, but the concierge has got to go."

"Did you hear Blossom is going to work for a nudist colony in Florida."

Booboo gasped.

"Are you kidding?" She asked.

"No. Some guy with a nudist resort in Florida stayed here a couple days, and Blossom went back with him."

"She's nothing but white trash," Booboo said. "What is the name of the resort?"

"Some guy named Benny. That's all I know."

"Tell Jeff that I want him to check out solar panels, and let me know what it would cost to convert to solar heat if you would, please," Booboo said.

"Okay, sure."

"Thanks, Susie."

Mrs. Higgins left a five dollar bill on the counter and walked to the lobby.

"Hello, Mrs. Higgins," Danny said to her as she walked past him to the front desk.

"Hello," she said smugly.

"May I see the sign-in for the past couple weeks, please," she said to the front desk clerk.

Mrs. Higgins stood at the desk and leafed through.

"Do you have a piece of paper and pen, please?" she asked.

She took the pen and paper and made notes as she looked down the pages. She wanted to know who Blossom had met at her hotel. She was looking for Florida plates and found only a couple and made a note of them. One was Benny Goodwin. She knew who he was. That asshole, she thought. He was doing that to spite her. She had met him at a party one of her friends in Florida on New Year's Eve. It was just a quickie, but she hadn't entirely written him off. Not that it mattered now. She wadded up the paper in her hand but didn't discard it. She didn't need any more office gossip.

CHAPTER 28

Cindy got back home from property inspection around five o'clock and brought pizza for dinner.

"I have to pick up Blossom at the airport this evening. Do you want to ride to the airport with me?"

"May I go to the gym, please?"

"I don't think so. She's supposed to be there at seven, but what if the plane doesn't get there on time? I don't want to have to leave to come and get you and then have to go back again. It's too far."

"I could walk back home," Jason said.

"No, honey. That's too far for you to walk. We can watch the planes land. Wouldn't you like to do that?"

"Okay. I guess so," Jason said.

After finishing Jason's homework and the pizza they left for the long drive to the airport and parked in the parking lot nearest the baggage claim. Cindy smiled when she thought maybe Blossom wouldn't have any luggage. She and Jason went inside and sat and watched through the plate glass as planes took off and landed.

"Did you learn about the sound barrier yet in school?"

"No. What is that?" Jason asked.

"It's when a plane goes so fast it breaks the sound barrier, when it goes faster than the speed of sound, at 767 miles per hour. This airport is named after the man who broke the sound barrier for the first time in 1947," she said. "Chuck Yeager."

"Chuck Yeager is a pilot?"

"Yes."

"They can't do that in a car, can they?" Jason asked.

"Maybe they can now, but not back then. There's Blossom's plane. See the Delta plane pulling in?"

They watched and saw Blossom walking from the plane to the lower level where she walked back up into the main lobby and saw Cindy and Jason waiting.

"Hey, guys. Thanks for coming for me," she said.

"How was your trip?" Cindy asked.

"It was nice."

"Do you have any luggage?" Cindy asked.

"This is all I brought," Blossom said with her carry-on and purse at her side.

"Great. How was your flight?"

"It was good, no problems."

"How was your trip to the beach?" Blossom asked.

"Great. The weather was perfect."

They drove back to the trailer park making small talk with Jason and pulled up in front of Blossom's trailer to let her out.

"Here we are, home again," Cindy said.

"Here's some money for gas and parking," Blossom said and shoved it into the compartment below the ash tray of her car.

"Thanks. We'll talk later," Cindy said. "I can come by and clean for you tomorrow if you'd like."

"I'll call you," she said.

"Okay. Goodnight."

Blossom leaned down and looked in at Jason sitting in the back seat.

"See you later handsome."

"Bye, Blossom," Jason said and smiled at her.

Early the next morning after Cindy got back from taking Jason to school and was having a cup of coffee reading the paper her phone rang.

She didn't get calls early in the morning usually. Maybe someone was calling about her new listing, she thought and answered.

"Hello. This is Cindy."

"Hello. Cindy Hart?"

"Yes, this is she," Cindy said.

"This is Lieutenant Paul Miller with the State Police. I'm sorry to bother you, but a car like yours was reported to have been used in a sodomy-rape case last Tuesday, and I need to ask you where you were."

"I was at the Holiday Inn at Nags Head with a friend all last week. As far as I know my car was parked in my driveway here at the trailer park the whole time I was gone. It was here when I got back parked the same place I left it."

"I had to ask," he said.

"Well, now you know."

"Thank you." He said and hung up.

"Asshole," she said and hung up.

Then the phone rang again, and she jumped.

"Hello," she said.

"Cindy, this is Doctor Jones' office. I'm calling to remind you of your appointment this afternoon at two p.m."

"Thanks for reminding me," she said. "I'll be there."

CHAPTER 29

Cindy was nervous about her appointment and considered cancelling it. She had slept so well with Chuck even though she hadn't taken any sleeping pills and wasn't used to actually sleeping with anyone. She felt more relaxed than she had for a long time, and there hadn't been any hallucinations for several days. Maybe it was exhaustion, and now things would be better. She knew she would miss Chuck, and her heart broke a little, but it probably wouldn't have worked out between them anyway. He was a player, and she didn't even know what that meant.

After Jason's dad got killed in such a terrible accident she cried like a baby and was a wreck for months during her pregnancy. After Jason was born she recovered. She still sometimes wondered if she would have gotten married if he hadn't been killed. It wasn't exactly a done-deal, and now it seemed like history repeating itself, another apparent dead-end. She didn't know what to think about that. Apparently she was destined to be a single parent.

She decided to keep her appointment. Dr. Jones was an older guy and very reserved and formal acting. He wore a suit and vest with a tie and had short salt and pepper hair and wire-rimmed glasses. He was tall and thin as a spider. His name plate on his desk said Harry A. Jones,

MD. She sat on a leather chair next to his desk as he made notes onto a pad then asked her if it would be alright if he recorded their sessions.

"I suppose so, as long as they're private and no one else listens to them," she said.

"No one else will be listening to them," he said and turned on the recorder.

"Are you taking any medications?" he asked.

"I have a prescription for sleeping pills and an anti-depressant medication."

"Tell me what the problem is."

"I've been hallucinating."

"Tell me about the hallucinations. When did they start? How often do you experience them? Do you hear voices?"

"I started seeing things a couple months ago, but no voices. It's happened a few times."

"What kinds of things are you seeing?"

"I noticed a guy's face looking like a rat-face at the office where I work. He's the manager and has a glass office, so I can see him in there, and one day he looked at me, and he had a rat face. That has happened few times. Also, I saw a guy that looked like a homeless man walking up the street, and he looked like a guy I know who isn't homeless and doesn't have that kind of appearance. I'm sure it wasn't him, but it looked exactly like him. It's like a flashbulb goes off, and I see things that aren't really there. Also, I have a reoccurring dream, a nightmare really. I wake up and someone has their arms around me from behind, wrapped around me real tight, so tight I can't move. I struggle to get away bending his hands back, but it's like there are no bones in his hands, like rubber hands, and I can't pry loose. I very seldom sleep with anyone, so I don't know why I think someone is in bed with me. It's very scary. I don't know who it is. I think maybe it's an alien, one of those grays. Finally I jerk myself awake, and I'm in my own bed, alone."

"Do you have any children?"

"I have one son. He's eight years old."

"Did you have a normal childbirth?"

"Yes. I've always been fairly healthy. Other than having my tonsils out and having a baby, I've never been hospitalized or had to take medication much."

"Are you married?"

"No. My son's father was killed in a car wreck when I was pregnant. We weren't married."

"Are your parents living? Do you have brothers and sisters?"

"My parents are living. I have an older brother. He lives in Cleveland."

"Did you go to college?"

"I went a couple years, but I dropped out. I got my real estate license instead."

"How is your son doing in school?"

"He's doing great. My parents keep him in the summers, and we usually spend weekends with them."

"So you and Jason and your parents get along with no problems?"

"Most of the time. Mom and Dad used to fight when we were kids, but now they seem like best friends, and they adore Jason."

"What does your father do for a living?"

"He's an English teacher."

"Is your mother a stay-at-home mom?"

"She works part-time selling cosmetics," Cindy said.

"Did you have problems at work getting along with others?"

"No. I mean sometimes I think they're stuck up, but nothing much. I've never had hallucinations before. That worries me."

"Do you use recreational drugs?"

"I smoke pot sometimes on weekends and have a few drinks, nothing major."

"Are you dating anyone?"

"I was seeing someone, but he had to go to prison for racketeering. You may have read about it in the newspaper. His name is Chuck Floyd. I didn't meet him until a few months ago, and I didn't know anything about it. We said goodbye, though. He said for me not to wait on him or come to see him, that I need to care for my son."

"He sounds like a reasonable guy. How about the real estate business? How's that going?"

"Great. I'm doing as well as anyone else right now. I sold a couple commercial buildings recently, and I have a few good listings."

"Is sex good for you?"

"Sex was fine; past tense, I'm afraid."

"Do you use birth control?"

"Yes."

"I'd like to run a few tests on you."

"What kind of tests?"

"Allergy tests, blood tests" he said. "You could be allergic to something. Sometimes people become allergic to something they weren't allergic to before. It might be causing your symptoms."

CHAPTER 30

It was raining hard that morning, and Cindy didn't feel like getting soaked going to the office. She wanted to ask Blossom about Chuck, anyway, but since Blossom and Jack were no longer seeing one another, she probably wouldn't know anything about it. Cindy thought maybe if she could just find out where Chuck was she could get him off her mind. She smoked a cigarette and watched out the bay window as the rain hit the road and splashed into the mud puddles. The trees were full and green, and the lilac was in bloom. Suddenly she saw something, and the cigarette fell from her mouth and landed on her lap.

It was a grotesque-looking creature about four feet tall walking up the road in the rain. His legs seemed to go outward away from his body as he wobbled clumsily undeterred by the rain. He looked like one of those gargoyles, she thought and picked the cigarette up off her lap, used for rain gutters in medieval times whose mouths opened up so that the water would shoot out of their mouths. It had disappeared into the rain and misty fog when she looked back up. She wondered if it was really there, even somewhere in another reality or dimension, but the fact was her brain wasn't functioning properly. The cigarette burned a hole in her tee shirt, and it was smoldering. She jumped up and pulled her shirt off and threw it into the sink and poured water over it. She hoped no one could see her through the window dancing around like a crazy person on fire. She then went to the bathroom and took a shower and dressed for the office. There was no sense in sitting around there imagining things, she thought.

When she pulled into the parking lot she saw Jack get out of his El Dorado and run into the side door of the hotel near the restaurant. She thought maybe she would have breakfast there, too, and maybe Jack would tell her something about Chuck. She got out of the car with her umbrella in hand and went to the side door and walked up the hallway past the vending machines and then into the restaurant, but she didn't see Jack anywhere. The bar didn't open until later in the day even though you could see it on the other side of the restaurant when the curtains were pulled open in the evening for dinner. She didn't think he'd be in there. He may have gone to the restroom, she thought, or maybe he went to Booboo's office.

She walked back down the hallway and stopped just short of the doorway and listened. She could hear him talking and listened. She determined that he must be on the phone. She could hear him now. He seemed agitated about something and raised his voice.

"I don't give a damn if you have to beat his ass to get it, just get my hundred dollars back off that little weasel. He knew which trailer it was. I said twenty-seven, not twenty-nine. That's not my fault."

Those words hit Cindy like a ton of bricks. Her trailer number was twenty-seven, and Blossom's was twenty-nine. Apparently Jack had given someone a hundred dollars to spray-paint WHORE onto the side of her trailer rather than Blossom's trailer. She took a step backwards away from the door to catch her breath. She felt like she was going to faint. She couldn't make a scene. Her knees began to buckle, and she quickly turned around and walked to the ladies room and went into a stall and sat down with her head between her legs hoping she wasn't going to pass out. Her heart was pounding and her hands were shaking. Why, she thought. Why would he do that, or want to do that to her? She went to the water basin and washed her hands and splashed water onto her face. I ought to kill that no-good, son-of-a-bitch, she thought. When Cindy walked into the real estate office all eyes were on her.

"Hi, Cindy," Irene said. "How are you today?"

"I'm okay," she said.

"You look like a drowned kitten," Irene said.

"Are you alright?" Helen asked.

They were really a little concerned about her. Her hair was messy, and her face looked wet and flushed.

"No, I'm fine. I just ran from the car in the rain," she said.

She realized she had left her umbrella in the bathroom stall. She sat down and opened up her MLS book and took a deep breath trying to remain calm.

"How are you guys doing today? What's new and exciting?" she asked trying to change the subject.

"Nothing much," Irene said. "I got a new listing. I want you to sell it, Cindy."

"Where is it?" Cindy asked.

"It's over on the west side on Hilltop Road. It's a four-bedroom with two and a half baths, a great-room with cathedral ceilings, a finished basement with a recreation room, a detached three-car garage, and two stone fireplaces. It's got hardwood floors and carpet in the basement. They're asking $255,000. It's an acre lot, a little steep, not much mowing required. It's all landscaped with shrubbery and trees and has a little running water pond in back. It's a real nice place."

Cindy listened trying to block out the static in her head.

"I don't know if any of my people can go up that high. I'll call and see what they say, though. Is anyone living there now?"

"No, it's empty. There's a lockbox on it. He got a transfer with a big pay increase, so the price may be negotiable. He needs to sell it, but he won't have to give it away. His wife died a year ago."

"Have you heard anything about Chuck?" John asked.

"No. Why? Have you?" she asked.

"I heard they took him to South Central Jail. He'll be transferred out of there, though. That's just a holding tank."

"Chuck and I agreed that it would be best under the circumstances if we didn't continue to see one another," she said. "He seemed like a good guy to me, but there are other fishes in the sea."

"That's right, Cindy," Irene said. "You can do better."

"He's not the marrying kind," Dottie said. "He's always carrying on with first one and then another."

The office secretary answered the phone.

"It's for you, Cindy," she said. "It's Blossom."

Cindy answered the phone.

"Hello. Sure. Okay. Bye," she said.

"What's Blossom doing now that she doesn't have a job?" John asked.

"She may be moving to Florida. She went down there for a job interview. We're going to have lunch."

Cindy wanted to get what Jack said off her mind, and Chuck off her mind. She called her prospect and told her about the new listing on Hilltop saying it was listed for more than what she and her husband were looking for, but they could make an offer. Irene listened.

"He might even do owner financing," she said.

"You may ask for owner-financing," Cindy said. "Two o'clock is fine. I'll drive. I know where it is. Okay. Bye."

"I hope you sell it," Irene said.

Cindy smiled and started organizing her briefcase with the proper contract forms. She wondered if Jack had gone into the restaurant for breakfast yet. She walked back out into the lobby and back to the restaurant and looked again. He was sitting at the coffee bar. She walked up nonchalantly and sat beside him. He looked over at her wondering why someone was sitting so close when there were other stools available. He recognized her then and knew she must want to ask him about Chuck.

"Hello, Jack," she said.

"Hello, Cindy. How are you?" he asked.

"I'm alright."

The waitress came and brought Jack's breakfast, and Cindy asked for a coffee.

"I'm really going to miss Chuck," she said.

"Yep. Me, too," he said.

"I'm sure. He was practically a permanent fixture at the gym, wasn't he?"

"Just about. Chuck's a popular guy. I hate the thoughts of him in prison, but he can take care of himself. That's for sure."

"I heard he's at South Central."

"That's right," Jack said.

Cindy thought about whether to mention she knew who painted Blossom's trailer and take him up on his thousand dollar offer. Jack started eating his breakfast, and Cindy sipped on her coffee. Then she got some money out of her purse and laid it on the counter.

"You don't have to run off," Jack said.

"I have to get back to work. Blossom and I are having lunch today."

"Tell her to come by my office tonight. I'm going to an auction in Virginia this afternoon. I won't be back until late tonight. Tell her I'll be at the bar around midnight. I owe her some money."

"Okay. Sure, I'll tell her. What kind of auction is it?"

"It's an estate auction."

"That sounds interesting. I'll give Blossom the message."

Cindy walked back to her office. Mark had come in.

"Hey, Mark," Cindy said.

"Hello, Cindy."

"Did you close on Mrs. Romeo yet?"

"The closing is next week."

"I haven't heard back from Joey, but I think he's counting on part of the profit from that sale to buy the apartment building."

"Someone made an offer on the apartment building, but they haven't accepted it yet," Mark said.

"How do you know?" Cindy asked.

"I called about it. I showed it, but they didn't want to offer as much as the other offers. Four hundred thousand is what I heard.

"I'd better get ahold of Joey and let him know," Cindy said and picked up the phone and dialed.

"Hello, Joey. This is Cindy Hart. I need to let you know there's an offer on the apartment building at $400,000. If you want to make an offer on it, you should do it soon. I'm here at the office now," she said.

By lunchtime Cindy had sold the apartment building to Joey Romeo for $405,000. The office was buzzing when Blossom walked in.

"Hi, all you real estate moguls," Blossom said over top the buzz.

Everyone turned to see her. She was stunning in a white backless jumpsuit with the straps that crisscrossed in front. John and Irene looked at one another with raised eyebrows. Bob with Joe and Dottie looked through the window.

"Hello, Blossom," Cindy said. "Love your outfit!"

"Me, too," John said. "You look like a million bucks."

"Hi, Blossom," Irene said. "How are you?"

"I'm doing great," she said. "So what's new with you guys?"

"I hear Mrs. Higgins isn't too thrilled with the concierge or us, for that matter," Irene said.

"She isn't very smart," Blossom said. "I hope you're hungry, Cindy, because I'm starved."

"I am hungry as a bear," Cindy said.

"Where did Danny work before?" Irene asked Blossom.

"He works part-time at the Civic Center," she answered.

"Where are you girls having lunch? Here?" John asked.

Blossom and Cindy wanted to have a private conversation and hedged a little.

"Not sure," Blossom said. "I'd like to have a milkshake and a cheeseburger and fries. Doesn't that sound good?"

"That does sound good," Cindy said.

"That's exactly what I was thinking. You read my mind," John said.

"I'm buying," Mark said.

Cindy and Blossom giggled.

"What do you say, ladies?" Mark asked.

"Okay," Blossom said. "If you'll behave yourselves."

"Anyone else want to have lunch with us?" Cindy asked and looked around the room.

"No, I'm going home," Irene said. "But I'll be back by the time you get back from showing the house on Hilltop, just in case."

"I've got too much to do," Dottie said. "Thanks, anyway."

"Come along, Pilgrims," John said.

"Where to?" Blossom asked.

"I'll drive," Mark said.

"Where's Helen?" Cindy asked.

"She has jury duty."

"Oh, that's right. I forgot about that."

Cindy and Blossom followed the guys to Mark's Cadillac. Blossom and Cindy got in the back seat, and John sat up front.

"I'm glad it stopped raining for a minute, anyway," Blossom said.

"It was pouring earlier. I was about drowned going into the office this morning," Cindy said. "They said I looked like a drowned rat."

Cindy took her compact from her purse and put on some lipstick and flicked her hair with her fingers.

"Dag! No wonder. I forgot to put on any makeup," she said, "and my hair looks like a bird's nest."

"Cindy, you look like that actress in The Birds," Mark said.

"Oh, thanks. After the birds landed on her head and picked her brains, I'm sure," Cindy said and laughed.

"Here, let me comb your hair. It's sticking up a little," Blossom said and reached for the comb and took it out of Cindy's hand.

"I need all the help I can get," Cindy said.

"There you go, that's better," Blossom said and gave her back the comb.

They went inside and sat at a table and ordered cheeseburgers and fries. The restaurant was decorated like Happy Days, and the jukebox was playing an old Buddy Holly song.

"Are you really moving to a nudist colony, Blossom?" John asked.

"I think so. I got a pretty good offer."

"An offer you can't refuse?" John asked.

"You could say that."

"I won't have a good neighbor if you move away, Blossom," Cindy said.

"I will miss you, too, Cindy," Blossom said, "and Jason. Cindy's little boy is so precious. I love him."

"He's a sweetheart, isn't he?" Cindy said.

"He sure is." Blossom said.

"He loves to go to the gym and play basketball," Cindy said, "but he does his homework first. He makes good grades. If he can keep it in his pants, we'll be okay, I think."

"Isn't that the truth," John said. "My boys are fourteen and sixteen. That's when things get tricky, when they start wanting to drive."

"Mine are sixteen and seventeen," Mark said. "They're hell on wheels."

"Do they have girlfriends yet?" Cindy asked.

"They think they do," Mark said. "It's in their heads."

"I'll bet you were a heart breaker back in the day," Blossom said to Mark and winked when he glanced over at her.

"In my day? What do you mean by that? I can still do what I used to do all night, and it only takes me about five minutes.

"My wife knows karate," John said. "She can beat my ass."

"She knows karate? Really?" Cindy asked.

"She can bust a cinder block."

"My wife's into voodoo," Mark said. "She has the mark of the beast."

Cindy and Blossom laughed.

"You guys," Cindy said. "You crack me up."

"What is up with Danny? He wears lipstick and winks at me when I walk by," John said.

"I think he's AC/DC," Cindy said. "He seems nice. I like him. I hope Mrs. Higgins doesn't fire him."

"Me, too," Blossom said. "He needs the job."

CHAPTER 31

At two o'clock in the afternoon Cindy was chauffeuring her couple to the house on Hilltop. The streets were all steep on the west side of Main Street to a more prestigious area of low-upper-class homes. Some sat way back away from the streets and were almost never on the market, handed down to the rightful heirs. The couple sat in the back seat and was very quiet.

"The streets are kept up real good in the winter over here. As you can see, they would have to be, otherwise traffic would not be able to stop on Main Street, and no one could get in or out," Cindy said. "The school is just a couple blocks away."

The couple made no comment, but she could hear a bit of resolve in their breathing. She pulled up in front of a white brick with dark brown split shingles then pulled into the driveway and parked. There were red maple trees lining the back of the property and a couple dogwoods on each side of the home.

"Are your kids both in high school?" Cindy asked.

"Yes," the lady answered.

"Shall we?" Cindy said and motioned for them to follow.

She went to the side door where the lockbox was located and went in through the pantry room which led to the kitchen.

"If I had parked in the garage, we could have used the back door which goes right into the master bedroom. If you have groceries, of course, this would be the way to enter into the pantry and kitchen. The front door opens into an entryway, and there's a back door."

The couple walked slowly through the house and whispered to each other not saying much aloud to Cindy. The windows that wrapped around one corner of the house in the dining room appealed to them. When they got back to the master bedroom and saw the huge master bathroom with a sunken tub and a view to an enclosed rose garden, though, she gasped.

"Isn't it beautiful? I love that. I can only imagine the roses in bloom."

"It sure is," Cindy said. "If there is anything you have a question about, anything you'd like to see again, just say so. Let's walk outside."

Cindy opened the door to the garage, and they walked into the garage and out the garage doors so Cindy could show them that the garage doors worked properly then led them to the garden area and opened the gate to see inside.

"See. I'd probably run a clothes line through here and hang up my laundry to dry. I love the smell of line-dried clothes in the summer," Cindy said.

"My mother always hung our clothes out to dry," the lady said.

"This is a little out of our price range, though," the man said.

"You sold a house before moving here, didn't you?" Cindy asked.

"Yes, but we still owed a lot on it," he said.

"If you could put down a good down payment, the owner may finance at a lower interest rate."

"That might work. Do you have an idea of how much the payments would be?" he asked.

"If you put down $30,000 on this house, you could get the payments down to about a thousand a month for thirty years if he will accept $230,000, that is. That's about four and half percent interest which is better than you could get at the bank right now."

"Do you know what their utility bills run?" he asked.

"Yes. It has gas heat which was three-hundred a month on a budget. The electric bill varied but averaged out around seventy-five a month."

"What are the taxes?" he asked.

"A couple thousand a year."

They walked quietly around the rest of the yard, and he drifted off to himself and looked down at the neighboring properties and stood.

"Have you looked at many houses yet?" Cindy asked.

"Yes. We've looked at a lot of houses," she said.

"Are you from India?" Cindy asked.

"Yes. My husband is from Sri Lanka. We met at the University of Virginia."

"He's an engineer at DuPont, isn't he?"

"Yes."

"What is your job?" Cindy asked.

"I'm a doctor of neurology at General Hospital," she said and smiled, "since last week. We are so anxious to get out of the apartment. It is so noisy, and we have no place to park, but we want to feel at home."

"This would be convenient to both your jobs," Cindy said. "I have to tell you that I was only going by what the listing agent was saying about the seller and his motivation. He may or may not accept owner financing. I know your husband said to stay around $200,000, but if you think this is the house for you, we should consider making an offer right away."

The husband came back up to them and nodded his head yes. Cindy started walking toward the car, and they followed talking softly together a few feet behind her. She was on a roll.

CHAPTER 32

It was almost five o'clock before Cindy completed the offer. Irene said she would present it to the seller as soon as possible and have an answer by the following day. That evening Cindy called Blossom.

"Hey, Blossom. I'm sorry we didn't get to talk much today. I really wanted to ask you about your trip."

"I wanted to ask you about your trip, too. Did you have a nice time at the beach?"

"Yes. It was just what the doctor ordered," Cindy said. "I miss Chuck, though."

"I can imagine. I haven't seen or heard from Jack at all, but I did mail him his stupid Medicare card. Booboo probably had a hissy fit."

Cindy laughed and thought about whether to tell her what Jack said.

"Are you going back to Florida?" Cindy asked.

"I've been writing down the pros and the cons on a legal pad trying to make up my mind. The thing is I don't know what to do with this trailer. I'm afraid it'll get vandalized if I just leave it here."

"You could keep it and later if you decide to make it permanent, then put it in the paper for sale. I'll help you sell it."

"I may look for another job around here this week, and if I don't find a good job, then I'll move to Florida," she said. "I really won't have much choice."

"You could apply at the Hampton. Did Jack give you a letter of reference?"

"No. I didn't ask. Booboo would have to type it."

"I'll type one for you tomorrow," Cindy said. "I'll even ask Jack to sign it next time I see him."

"Okay. Thanks," Blossom said. "Was Chuck very depressed?"

"He didn't seem depressed to me. Not like I would be if I had to go to prison."

"I can't imagine. I saw him at the bowling alley a couple weeks ago. I stopped in there on Saturday night and watched Jack and him bowl. That woman Chuck left when he bought the duplex from you was there, Priscilla. She and some other woman sat there and chain smoked and drank beer. She has three-inch claws. He didn't pay any attention to her at all. I watched to see, but he acted like she wasn't even there."

"Did you leave before Jack and Chuck did?"

"Yes but I waited in the parking lot until Jack and Chuck walked out. I waited and watched to see if Priscilla came outside and followed him. She didn't. I don't think either one of them saw me. What did Chuck do with the duplex? Did he just leave it?"

"His sister is there now," Cindy said. "He said she leased it from him and the grill."

"Wow. I didn't know he had a sister."

"She moved here from Ohio. Her husband died a year ago. She gets his pension and social security. He said she wants to work, though."

"That's good."

"I appreciate you checking on Jason this evening. I'll clean for you as soon as I get a chance," Cindy said.

"Don't worry about it. I haven't been here to dirty the place up much."

"Okay. I'd better get Jason to bed. I'll talk to you later," Cindy said and hung up.

"Come on, Jason. It's time for bed," she said.

"Okay. Can you read me a story, Mom?"

"Sure, Baby."

She pulled down the covers on Jason's bed, and he crawled in as she tucked him in and sat down on the edge of the bed beside him. There were books inside a shelf in the headboard of his bed. She pulled one out and opened it and began to read. In a few minutes Jason was sound asleep. She looked at Jason sleeping and was a little envious. He could grow up to be anything he wanted to be. He could go to college and meet a girl and get married and have a family. Her life was so fragile, so precarious, like standing on the edge of a cliff in a hurricane. Despite making a big commission that day, and maybe another one tomorrow, it was not a secure position. She leaned down and kissed Jason before turning off the light. She wondered what Nikki was doing and decided to call her. She sat down with a glass of wine and dialed Nikki.

"Hello, Nikki. I missed seeing you this weekend. Are you busy?"

"No. I'm glad you called. How was your vacation?"

"It was real nice. We weren't exactly celebrating, but we had fun."

"Did he move to Florida?"

Cindy had forgotten that's what she told Nikki. There was no reason to tell her otherwise. She wouldn't want it to get back to her parents.

"Yes. I think my neighbor, Blossom, is moving to Florida, also. How are you doing?"

"I'm doing very nicely. Making enough money to pay the bills anyway," Nikki said.

"That's all that matters," Cindy said

"You sound a little down," Nikki said.

"I sold an apartment building today. I'll make about $10,000 on that one sale."

"Wow, Cindy. That's great. I'd be jumping up and down with joy."

"The real estate market is not very dependable, though," Cindy said. "It's feast or famine."

"Make hay while the sun shines," Nikki said.

"I heard Cecil died," Cindy said. "Who do they think did it?"

"Frank and Jay think Cecil probably did it himself. He was depressed. Cecil's wife and Mr. Hamrick were having an affair which started maybe even before his wife died. Cecil knew about it. He was trying to get Mr. Hamrick fired, but they were going to let Cecil go is what I heard. That was dirty of the bank."

"I agree," Cindy said.

"Someone must have made that bomb, though. I'll bet it was a coal miner with access to explosives. Cecil probably said he was going to blow up a rock or something, and no one is going to admit to it now."

"You're right. You're so smart, Nikki. I love you," Cindy said.

"I love you, too. Are you coming home on Friday or Saturday?"

"I'm not sure yet. Is Jeremy with his dad this weekend?"

"Yes, he has him Friday and Saturday night, but maybe we can all go to the lake on Sunday and have a picnic."

"That would be nice. I'll see you, later, alligator," Cindy said.

"Sleep tight, don't let the bedbugs bite."

Cindy hung up the phone and turned on the television. It was already after eleven o'clock. She felt restless and wondered if she should call Blossom back and let her know what Jack said. It kind of slipped her mind. She had been avoiding thinking about the entire subject ever since she overheard what he said. She thought she probably shouldn't tell Blossom any of it. Suddenly the television was talking to her, calling her by name.

"Cindy. We've been trying to reach you, Cindy. Remember the gun Chuck gave you? Go get it. Take it to the Hotel. Jack is there. You have to kill him."

Cindy walked to her bedroom. A Smith and Wesson was hidden in a clothes hamper in the dirty clothes. She pulled it out and walked back to the living room and looked at the television. Someone she didn't recognize was looking back at her.

"Are you with the FBI?" she asked. "Are you doing this?"

"Yes. I'm with the FBI," he said. "We have control of your television."

She set the gun down and looked for her shoes. It was raining again. She took out a pair of loafers and then put on her raincoat. She got a scarf out and wrapped it snuggly around her head then tiptoed into Jason's room to make sure he was sleeping soundly. He looked like an angel, so peaceful. She put the gun inside her purse, put on her shoes and left quietly.

CHAPTER 33

Cindy drove to the railroad tracks behind Higgins Hotel and parked out of sight. The railroad tracks set back away from the hotel about a hundred feet. The houses on the other side of the tracks were down an incline another hundred feet. It was very foggy and visibility was only a few feet. There were a couple cars parked at the back of the building. She looked inside each one to make sure no one was inside. The cars were empty, and no one was around. She walked slowly to the back of the hotel listening carefully and looked around the corner to see if Jack's car was parked there. The light at the back entrance lit up the side parking area, and she could see Jack's El Dorado parked near the door. She thought he was probably waiting inside the bar thinking Blossom would be there. A couple left the bar laughing as they walked out into the night air holding hands and drove off on their merry way. Cindy had the gun underneath her arm holding it with her right hand and waited.

The door opened again and Cindy peered from around the edge of the back of the building. It was Jack, and he strolled toward his car.

"Jack," she said loud enough for him to hear her.

He turned on his heel and looked around then walked to the back of the building and peered around the corner to see Cindy standing there.

"Hello, Jack," Cindy said.

"Cindy? What the hell are you doing?" he asked. "Is Blossom with you?"

"No, Jack, it's just me. I have to ask you something. Do you remember telling me that if I could find out who painted WHORE on Blossom's trailer that you would give me a thousand dollars?"

"Yes. Did you find out?" he asked.

"Yes."

"Who was it?" he asked.

"It was you, Jack," she said.

Jack laughed but wondered how she knew.

"You must have eavesdropped on me talking on the phone, you little tramp. You're just white trash after all," he said with a sneer in his voice. "You should have taken me up on my offer."

Cindy pulled out the gun and shot before Jack had a chance to walk away. The bullet hit him between the eyes. He crumpled to the ground, and she ran quickly back to her car and drove away. When she crossed the bridge she threw the gun over into the river and then stopped for a pack of cigarettes at the 7-11 before going back home. She slept very soundly and didn't wake until Jason woke her the next morning.

"Mom, wake up! It's time to get up," Jason said.

"Okay, Sweetie. I'm getting up."

CHAPTER 34

Cindy fed Jason breakfast and took him to school as usual. When she got back home she turned on the news and heard that Jack Higgins was found shot dead at Higgins Hotel. Cindy walked to Blossom's and knocked on her door thinking that she may still be in bed, but she should tell her about Jack. Cindy knocked again more loudly. Blossom came to the door in her nightgown with a puzzled look on her face.

"Turn on the news," Cindy said. "Turn on your television to the news."

"What?" Blossom said.

"Just turn on the news and listen." Cindy said.

"What happened?" Blossom asked and walked over and turned on the TV.

"What happened?"

"It's on the news now," Cindy said.

They stood in Blossom's living room and listened to the report. The police are investigating the shooting, and the cameras are on Higgins Hotel.

"What happened?" Blossom asked again.

"They said Jack Higgins was shot. He's dead."

Blossom screamed.

"Do you think Booboo did it?" Blossom asked.

"I have no idea," Cindy said.

"Oh, my God! I can't believe it," Blossom said.

"I'm sorry. I just thought you should know."

"I've been trying to decide whether to move to Florida. I should take this as a sign to move the hell out of here," Blossom said. "That shocked me!"

"I'm sorry. I should have lead up to it better," Cindy said

"It's not your fault. I'll make a pot of coffee. Sit down," Blossom said.

"I have to get ready and go to the office," Cindy said.

"Don't go to the office." Blossom pleaded.

"I have to." Cindy said. "I'll talk to you later. Come by and we'll have lunch."

CHAPTER 35

Cindy walked back to her trailer and took a shower and then called Irene to see if her couple's offer was accepted.

"Hi, Irene. I just wanted to see what your seller had to say about the offer on Hilltop," Cindy said.

"He doesn't want to owner finance," Irene said. "Did you hear about Jack Higgins?"

"Yes. It was on the news this morning."

"Someone saw him about two in the morning stretched out in the parking lot. They thought he was drunk, but he was dead, shot in between the eyes. He was at the bar and left around midnight, so he probably got shot as soon as he left the bar. Call me back after you talk to your couple," Irene said and hung up.

Cindy called her couple and gave them the news that the seller won't owner finance but will accept their offer.

"We'll have to initial the changes on the contract if you want to go forward," Cindy said.

In a little while they called her back and asked if the seller would accept ten thousand less if they can get financing on their own. Cindy relayed the message to Irene.

In a little while Irene called Cindy back and said if they can close right away. Everyone agreed, and Cindy asked her clients to meet her back at the office at noon to revise the contract. Cindy dressed for the office and went to meet her clients for their initials on the contract revisions. The office was quiet, and people seemed to be in a daze, but the show must go on. Everyone went on with the business at hand.

"Congratulations," Cindy said to her couple as they left the office smiling, pleased with their purchase.

Cindy handed the contract to Irene with the revisions initialed.

"Thank you, Cindy," she said.

"I bet Booboo will sell out and go back to Florida now. Just knowing someone killed him right here at their own establishment," Irene said.

"I don't think we'll have any problem getting financing for my couple. They've got about thirty or forty thousand from the sale of their previous home," Cindy said.

"They're getting a steal if you ask me," Irene said.

"I think so, too. Thanks, Irene, for another super listing. You're the queen!"

Irene smiled and placed the contract in her brief case.

"I have to fax this for his initials. Which bank are they going through?"

"City."

"I'll be afraid to leave here at night now," Irene said.

"When is the funeral?" John asked. "Does anyone know?"

"The wake is Thursday from six to eight, and the funeral is Friday at one," Irene said.

"Maybe Mrs. Higgins shot him," John asked.

"No," Irene said. "She isn't the type."

"Not the type? All women are the type," John said. "It's just boiling inside them until bang! And you're dead."

"Booboo fainted when the policeman came by and told her. They had to call an ambulance for her. She and Jack may have had their ups and downs, but she wouldn't have stayed married to him if she didn't love him," Irene said.

The secretary yelled.

"Cindy! You have a phone call, Cindy."

It was her doctor's office asking her to come in. Her test results were in and asked if she could be there at one on Friday, and she said she could and hung up.

"I have an appointment Friday at one," Cindy said to no one in particular. "I guess I'm not going to the funeral."

"Does Blossom know?" Irene asked Cindy.

"She saw it on the news, same as me," Cindy said.

"Want to go to lunch, Cindy?" Mark asked.

"No. I'm not hungry," she said. "I think Blossom is moving to Florida for that nudist job."

"Margaritaville, here she comes," John said.

"I might go with her," Cindy said. "Not really. I wouldn't do that to Jason. He sees enough of my ugly mug."

"Do Blossom's parents know?" Irene asked.

"Her parents are dead. She was adopted," Cindy said.

"Really," Helen said.

"Where are you going to eat, Mark?" John asked.

"Here, I guess. Anyone want to go to lunch?"

"I've already eaten," Dottie said.

"May as well," Irene said.

"Come Pilgrims, let us not perish," John said.

"Are you not going to eat, Cindy?" Mark asked.

"No. I don't feel hungry."

"What about a drink?" he asked.

Cindy breathed out a sigh.

"Okay," she said.

"Come Pilgrims, before we collapse of dehydration," John said.

They got up and walked to the restaurant together and sat at a table and had the crab soup except for Cindy who ordered a Tom Collins.

"I'm going to go back home and check on Blossom," she said. "She screamed."

"Did you tell her?" John asked.

"I told her to turn on the television after I heard it on the news. She turned white as a ghost."

When Cindy pulled in around four o'clock Blossom grabbed her purse and keys and pulled the locked door closed behind her and walked over to Cindy.

"I want to say goodbye before I leave for Florida," Blossom said.

"Now?" Cindy asked.

"Yes. I can't stand it. I can't stop thinking about Jack. I'll go crazy if I have to stay here."

"Oh, Blossom," Cindy said and hugged her. "Are you sure? Maybe you should wait."

"I want to give you my spare key," she said and handed it to Cindy, "just in case something might go wrong, or something."

"Okay," Cindy said.

"I'd like to say goodbye to Jason."

"Come on in," Cindy said.

They went inside, and Jason was sitting doing his homework.

"Hi, Jason," Blossom said.

"Hi, Sweetie," Cindy said. "Are you about finished with your homework?"

"Not yet."

"I'm moving to Florida, Jason. Can I give you a goodbye hug?" Blossom asked.

Jason stood up to hug her.

"I love you guys," Blossom said and stooped down and hugged him. "You be a good boy, Jason, and mind your mother."

"Okay," he said.

"You know you can always come back, Blossom," Cindy said.

"I know, but for now I think it would be best," she said.

"We'll miss you, won't we Jason?"

"Yes," Jason said and hugged her around the waist.

"I love you, Jason," she said. "I'm going to get going before I start crying."

"Call me when you get to Florida. Okay?" Cindy asked.

"Okay. Bye for now. I love you."

"I love you, too. Be safe."

Blossom walked back to her car and drove away as Cindy and Jason watched and waved as she drove out of sight.

CHAPTER 36

Cindy didn't go into the office on Friday but went directly to her doctor's appointment. He walked briskly into the office smiling.

"Its good news and bad news," he said. "You're allergic to metals, especially mercury. You have Multiple Chemical Sensitivity, MCS, so that explains your symptoms which we can deal with that. The bad news is if you have amalgam fillings, they may have to be removed and replaced with composite fillings."

"Really?"

"Do you have silver fillings?"

"A couple," she said.

"Do you eat seafood often?"

"Once a week."

"Don't eat Swordfish or Kingfish or Albacore White Tuna, and no more than six ounces of fish per week. Do you chew gum?" he asked.

"Yes, I chew gum."

"You should not chew gum until after the fillings are removed. It causes the mercury vapors from your fillings to be released and swallowed. Have you had anxiety attacks?"

"I'm not sure I'd even know, anymore, not lately," Cindy said.

"Coal-fired power plants have mercury emissions. That may be the main culprit considering the power plant is right across the river from you. You may need to move," he said. "Also, stay away from chemicals in cleansers, detergents, new carpet, car exhaust and cigarette smoke."

"I have been cleaning more than usual and smoking more than usual."

"Don't smoke, and tell your friends not to smoke. Buy cleansers without the chemicals. You can find them or make them yourself. Use vinegar instead of ammonia for example, and be diligent. Use more elbow grease instead of chemicals."

"I can't tell my friends not to smoke, but I can look into doing the other stuff. What about laundry detergent?" Cindy said.

"Buy the natural cleansers without the chemicals. Get an appointment with your dentist and let him know you're allergic to mercury. Have you had any more hallucinations?"

"The other day when it was raining real hard I saw a gargoyle walking up the road," Cindy said. "I don't know why, other than he may have fallen off someone's roof."

"I suppose that could happen," he said and looked at Cindy strangely. "Here's a list of the things you are allergic to and should avoid completely."

He handed her a sheet of paper with a long list.

"Wow. I'm allergic to a lot of things."

"Yes, but you can eliminate most of it without much inconvenience. I think you'll notice a difference right away."

"Thank you, Doctor."

He smiled at her and remembered that she was the one who was dating Chuck Floyd. He had gone to prison according to the paper.

"I'm sorry about your friend, Chuck Floyd," he said. "I read in the paper he got a couple years."

"I hadn't heard, but that sounds about right." she said.

"Ask the clerk to schedule you an appointment again in a month," he said.

"Okay," Cindy said. "Thank you."

CHAPTER 37

The days rolled by, and Cindy eliminated the items on her forbidden list and began to notice a difference, but she was still having that one reoccurring nightmare. Someone was in bed with her with their arms wrapped around her so tightly she could barely move, and no matter how hard she struggled to get away she couldn't. His hands felt like rubber that didn't have any bones in them. She tried to shake herself awake, and he asked her in plain English, What's your name? He talked normally, she thought. That was somewhat of a comfort.

She answered, Cindy. Then he said, My name is Evan. For a moment she was able to look back at him. His hair was finely combed strands of gold, and his beard was the same and flipped up on the ends around his chin. That was better than seeing an alien or some kind of monster. She thought he must live where there is no wind since his hair and beard were so neat with not a hair out of place, not even on his beard. If there was no wind, no one would need bones, she thought. She awoke with a little bit of peace for a change.

After the closing of her Indian couple who bought the Hilltop property she was particularly upbeat. It turned out to be one of her most gratifying sales, she thought. John watched Cindy and noticed she seemed happier and less lethargic.

"Cindy, you're in a cheerful mood," John said.

"I was just thinking of my Indian couple. They love that house, and their boys do, too."

"Have you heard from Blossom?" he asked.

"Yes. She called a couple nights ago. She says everyone is real nice to her, and everyone gets along fine."

"Is she working at that nudist camp?" Helen asked.

"It's a resort. I think they call themselves naturalists," Cindy said.

"Does everyone just go around naked?" Irene asked.

"Clothing is optional. She said about half of the people are usually nude. She said she missed clothes at first, but now she sometimes forgets she's even naked."

"I can't imagine going around with my ass shining," Helen said. "Can you?"

"Me, neither," Irene said. "I wouldn't like that at all. Bugs."

"Don't knock it unless you've tried it," Cindy said.

John and Mark laughed.

"Are you going to try it, Cindy?" Mark asked.

"I may take a vacation and check it out one of these days. How did your jury duty go, Helen?" Cindy asked.

"It was a murder trial," she said.

"Well, tell us about it," Cindy said. "I want to hear it."

"It was two different guys who murdered a guy they had met at a bar. We were hearing the case against just one of the guys, the other one had already been convicted. The old guy they murdered was buying them drinks and seemed to have money. The two guys asked the old guy to take them to Ohio. The old man said no, he didn't want to go to Ohio. They told him to take them as far as he was going and they'd get out and hitchhike. At some point the old man stopped the car to take a piss. The old man got out of the car, and they decided to rob him and take his car. They beat his brains out with a rock. We saw the photographs of him with his brains smashed out of his head. Then the two guys took his wallet which had about fifty dollars in it and took off in his car. They stopped and had pizza. How could anyone eat pizza after that?"

"They probably ordered it with extra cheese and sausage," John said.

"They were almost in Ohio and got stopped for speeding, and when the policeman asked for license and registration, he figured out the car didn't belong to them and arrested them."

"Not to mention they had drunk ten gallons of beer," Mark said.

"If they had gone just a little further and crossed the bridge into Ohio, they'd have gotten the death penalty."

"Wow. What makes people do shit like that?" Cindy asked.

"Could it be Satan?" Mark said.

"Yes, that's it," Cindy said. "You're right. That's what gets into people who do shit like that."

"Did they ever find out who made the bomb that blew up in the bank, Cindy?" John asked.

"No. They have a theory that a coal miner made the bomb and was just doing Cecil a favor, like he needed it to explode a rock on his property, but really Cecil was going to take it into Mr. Hamrick's office and blow him up or maybe he just decided to kill himself and wanted them to feel guilty. No one will confess to making the bomb now for fear of going to prison. His widow and Mr. Hamrick have sent out wedding invitations. I guess I'm going to go to it with my friend Nikki."

"That's nice," Irene said.

"What's nice about it? That stinks to high heaven," John said.

"I think he killed himself so his wife could get married again," Cindy said.

"Bullshit," Mark said.

"Well, anyway, they're getting married, and Nikki and I are going to it. It's as close to happily-ever-after as I can get," Cindy said.

Mrs. Higgins interrupted the conversation by quietly coming into the office and over to Helen's desk.

"Hello, Helen," she said. "How are you?"

"I'm doing well. How are you, Booboo?"

"I'm alright, thank you for asking. I'd like you to come by my office when you have some time. I'm going to sell the hotel and the gym."

"I'm not busy right now if you have the time," Helen said.

"Yes. Come on back to my office," Mrs. Higgins said.

Helen got up with her briefcase in hand and followed her. The other agents made eyes at each other.

"This is going to be interesting," Cindy said.

CHAPTER 38

Nikki had been extremely busy all day Saturday and was so tired she thought she probably wouldn't attend the wedding of Shelby and Mr. Hamrick. Cindy stopped by her shop that afternoon to convince her otherwise.

"You have to see your handy work," Cindy pleaded. "I want to see all the hair styles you created."

"Frank won't go. He said he wouldn't feel right about it," Nikki said.

"Well, apparently they feel right about it, and that's all that matters. Let's go shopping and buy new dresses," Cindy said.

"Do you have a walker? I'm so tired I'll need one," Nikki said.

Cindy laughed.

"Come on, let's go," Cindy said.

"Maybe I can find one at Good Will," Nikki said.

"Oh, please. I'll pay for it," Cindy said. "You won't even have to use your credit card."

"Oh, no," Nikki protested.

"Yes. I want you to come with me, so I'll buy your dress. No Good Will dresses, please."

"I'm still trying to get my tuition bill paid off," Nikki said.

"No problem. I have money to burn," Cindy said.

"On one condition, only if we can find it within an hour. I've been on my feet all day, and I'm exhausted."

"Okay. I know just where to look," Cindy said. "We can stop, and I'll buy your dinner, too."

They stopped at the mall and ran into Pennys. They looked quickly and found a couple dresses right away and tried them on.

"I love that color," Nikki said of Cindy's dress.

"Yes, me, too. See, ours match, sort of," Cindy said.

Cindy's was a powdery silver-blue empire waist, and Nikki's was a navy blue sheath which was short and strapless whereas Cindy's was long with halter straps.

"I love it," Nikki said. "I'll get some wear out of this one even with a jacket over it. I have navy heels that will look great. Thanks, Cindy."

"You're welcome. Now let's go get something to eat. I'm starving."

They went to a cafeteria style restaurant and ate heartily then Cindy dropped Nikki off and went back to her parent's house for the night. Her parents and Jason were watching a television show when she came in around ten o'clock. They all looked at her like they'd seen a ghost.

"What? Can't I come home early once in a while?" she asked.

"Yes, Dear," her dad said.

"What do you have there?" her mother asked.

"I bought a dress for the wedding tomorrow. Nikki and I went shopping. Are you guys going?"

"Your mother can if she wants. Jason and I are going treasure hunting."

"I don't think so," her mother said. "I want to go treasure hunting, too."

"I hope you find treasure," Cindy said. "Can I wear your black heels, Mom, the ones I like?"

"Yes, just don't take them home with you."

"Okay, thanks. I'm going to bed. It's been a long day. Goodnight," Cindy said.

"Good night, Mom," Jason said.

The next day Cindy woke up to a quiet and empty house. It was almost eleven o'clock. She could hardly believe she'd slept so late and couldn't remember ever having slept so long. She showered and sat down and ate a bowl of cereal. She felt like a new person. She loved the quiet where her parents lived beside the river. She could hear it gurgling when the television was off. There wasn't much traffic by there, and no one in the neighborhood ever mowed on Sundays. It was a neighborhood rule. Cindy put on her new dress and heels and called Nikki to let her know she was on her way.

At the wedding Nikki told Cindy the ones for whom she had done their hair and talked about the dresses. When the music started and Mrs. Pratt, the new Mrs. Hamrick started walking up the aisle with her son, there was an audible gasp. She looked so lovely in a vintage beige beaded dress along with a velvet cap and veil that came just below her eyes.

"Wow. She looks stunning," Nikki said.

"Did you do her hair?" Cindy asked.

"Yes. It looks good, doesn't it?" Nikki said.

"Yes. She looks great."

When the wedding ceremony was over, and everyone was leaving the church, Shelby looked back at Nikki and Cindy and smiled then tossed the bouquet. Cindy caught it but handed it to Nikki who backed off and wouldn't take it. People laughed at them trying to hand it off to each other, but Nikki refused it. Cindy turned around and threw it back into the crowd and ran. When they got back to Nikki's house Frank was there sitting on her front porch.

"Is that Frank?" Cindy asked.

"I wonder what he's doing," Nikki said.

Cindy parked and they walked together.

"Hello," Frank said. "How was the wedding?"

"It was nice," Nikki said. "What are you doing here?"

They walked up the steps onto the front porch, and Nikki got her keys out of her purse. Frank didn't answer. Maybe he didn't hear her, Nikki thought, as she let the keys jingle in from her hand.

"Were you waiting on me, Frank?" she asked.

"I took a walk and thought you'd be home soon so I stopped to wait and rest awhile."

"Oh."

"Hello, Frank," Cindy said.

"Hello, Cindy."

Nikki opened the door.

"Come on in, Frank," she said. "I want to change clothes. Cindy can get you guys a beer out of the fridge."

They walked in together, and Nikki went upstairs while Cindy walked into the kitchen. Frank sat down in the overstuffed recliner while Cindy opened a couple bottles of beer and brought one over to Frank.

"Here you go, Frank," she said.

"Thanks."

Cindy and he both took a long drink before Cindy walked over to the sofa and sat down.

"The air conditioning feels good," Cindy said.

"That sun is hot today. How was the wedding?" Frank asked.

"Shelby looked beautiful," Cindy said. "I didn't know she was so pretty. Nikki did her hair. It looked so good."

"Were there many guests?"

"The church was about half full, so that would be about a hundred people."

"Are you all going to the reception?" Frank asked.

"No, I'm not," Cindy said.

They could hear Nikki coming back down the stairs. She came around with a pair of shorts and a tee-shirt on in her bare feet.

"It sure feels good getting out of those clothes!" she said. "I was hot."

Cindy laughed.

"This dress isn't really too hot," Cindy said. "I don't have on nylons like you, that's the difference."

"I may have a pair of shorts and a tee-shirt that might fit you, Cindy."

"I should go on home," she said.

"Stay and have a hotdog. You don't have to run off."

Nikki went into the kitchen and got herself a beer and came back and sat on the sofa beside of Cindy and put her feet up on the coffee table.

"I bought a whole bag of shorts and tee-shirts the other day at a yard sale, Cindy. It's on the floor in my bedroom. I haven't even gone through them yet. Go see if you can find something."

Cindy set her beer on the coffee table then got up and walked upstairs then.

"Did you have a good time?" Frank asked Nikki.

"Sure. It was nice. You should have come."

"Was the FBI there?"

Nikki laughed.

"Of course not," she said.

"I figured they'd all be there with bells on."

"Nope. I doubt if they socialize much with their suspects."

"Aren't you going to the reception?"

"No, I just wanted to see her," Nikki said. "I'd rather have a hotdog and relax."

"Is that what you're having, hotdogs?" Frank asked.

"Yes. Are you hungry?" she asked.

"I could eat," he said.

"I'll grill us some dogs. I have a head of cabbage, too, and left-over chili. If you'll make the slaw," she said.

"Okay," Frank said. "Sure. Do you have chips?"

"I think so. I have frozen fries, too, if you want."

Cindy came back down the stairs and walked into the room wearing a pair of shorts and a tee-shirt in her bare feet then.

"Ta-dah," she said.

"Hey, you hit the jack pot!" Nikki said. "I like that tee-shirt. What does it say?"

"Margarittaville," Cindy said.

"Cool. I'm going to grill some hotdogs. Frank is going to make the slaw. Can you make some potato salad?"

"Sure. That sounds really good," Cindy said. "I need a margarita now."

"I have tequila and mix, enough for you a drink or two," Nikki said.

"Seriously? That would be great. Thanks, girlfriend."

Frank got up and walked into the kitchen and opened the refrigerator for the cabbage to make the slaw.

"Would you rather have a hamburger or a hotdog?" Nikki asked Cindy.

"A hotdog," Cindy said.

"Come on in the kitchen."

"When is Jeremy getting back?" Cindy asked.

"His dad is keeping him until bedtime, he said, around nine. I think they went to his moms today."

"Where is your slaw cutter?" Frank asked.

"I'll get it for you," Nikki said.

She pulled out a drawer full of utensils and handed Frank a slaw shredder.

"Do you put anything in your slaw besides cabbage?" he asked.

"Sometimes I put carrots in it," Nikki said. "I don't have any carrots, though."

"Do you have any onion?" Frank asked.

"I have onions. I'll chop one up," Nikki said.

"Here, I'll do it," Cindy said.

Nikki handed her an onion and took the wieners from the fridge and a container of chili.

"I'll warm up this chili. It's still good," she said.

"Do you want me to light the charcoal?" Frank asked.

"It's a gas grill," Nikki said.

Cindy started peeling the potatoes and Nikki looked in the cabinet and pulled out some buns, a fourth of a bottle of tequila, and a bag of chips and set them on the table.

"The mixer is in the fridge. I'm going to put on some music," Nikki said.

Nikki disappeared and in a few minutes the music started playing. Cindy put the potatoes on to boil then mixed herself a margarita. She started dancing to the music with her head back and her arms out from her sides when Frank came back into kitchen. He cleared his throat when he saw Cindy dancing, and she stopped and opened her eyes.

"Oh, Frank. Do you want a margarita?" she asked.

"No, thanks. I'll have another beer, though," he said.

Cindy opened the fridge and got Frank another beer and handed it to him. Then he sat back down to finish the slaw.

"What all do you put in your slaw?" Cindy asked.

"Mayo and a little vinegar, and a spoon full of sugar."

"Here's the sugar bowl," Cindy said and handed him the sugar.

"I need a spoon," he said.

Cindy handed him a spoon from the drawer, and Frank mixed up some dressing for the slaw. Nikki came back into the kitchen with a joint.

"We can take this out in the yard while we are grilling the meat. Get all the condiments and bring them out to the picnic table."

Nikki picked up a few of the bottles, and Cindy and Frank followed with the rest. They sat around the picnic table passing the joint for a few minutes.

"I'll finish the potato salad," Cindy said and went back to the kitchen. "I like it warm, do you all?"

"Yes, and put some mustard in it," Nikki said. "Do you like it that way, Frank?"

"Yes. I like it that way."

Nikki and Frank sat at the picnic table and drank their beers while Cindy made the potato salad.

Cindy brought out the potato salad and set it on the table and sat down with another margarita. Frank was taking the wieners off the grill. They sat and ate enjoying their hotdogs.

"Is Jay really running for sheriff?" Cindy asked.

"Yep. He's running for sheriff," Frank said.

"What do you have to do to run for Sheriff?" Cindy asked.

"File a fee and name a treasurer," Frank said. "We put up signs. Have you noticed them?"

"I saw one today," Cindy said. "I'm not registered to vote."

"You should register," Frank said. "Are you registered, Nikki?"

"Nope."

"You need to register to vote," he said.

"I have enough problems without trying to figure out who to vote for," she said.

"You little shits better register and vote for Jay. I'm his treasurer."

"La-tee-da," Nikki said and held the joint up into the air.

Cindy and Nikki started laughing then.

"What's funny?"

"Voting for Jay is kind of funny. I'm voting for this jay," Nikki said.

Cindy and Nikki laughed some more

"Oh, ha ha," Frank said. "Someone has to do it."

Nikki and Cindy tried to stop giggling. Nikki got up and started clearing the table and went back to the kitchen.

"I'm not a resident of this county," Cindy said.

"Well, you should still register and vote," Frank said.

"I have to be going. Jason is probably wondering what happened to me," she said.

Cindy got up from the table and walked back into the house. Nikki was cleaning the kitchen.

"I'm going to take off now. Thanks for going with me and for dinner," Cindy said.

"Are you okay to drive? I'll make you a cup of coffee first. Call Jason and tell him you'll be a little longer."

Nikki handed Cindy her phone, and she called.

"Hi, Jason. Did you have a nice treasure hunt? I'll be there to pick you up in about a half an hour. Be ready. I'll see you in a little while. Bye, Sweetie."

Nikki opened the door to the outside where Frank was still sitting and yelled out to him.

"Frank. Can you bring the rest of the food inside, please?"

Nikki's back yard was private, but the view was blocked by a detached garage on the alley behind her house to what would be an outstanding view of the mountain range behind them. Each side of her house was fenced with a tall privacy fence up to the front porch. She got the house when she and her husband divorced, and for that she was grateful.

"He's just sitting out there, reflecting, I guess," Nikki said.

"He seems like an alright guy," Cindy said.

"He's a little creepy," Nikki whispered.

"What do you mean?" Cindy asked.

"Just sitting on my porch like a zombie or something when I wasn't even home, is that not creepy? He didn't want to go to the wedding, but he sure wanted to know about it."

Nikki poured Cindy a coffee and herself one, also.

"That's not so creepy. If he'd been inside the house, that would be creepy," Cindy said.

Frank came back in carrying the potato salad and buns.

"Put the potato salad in the fridge, please," Nikki said.

"You guys have a good evening," Cindy said. "Don't do anything I wouldn't do."

"Don't forget your dress and shoes upstairs. Keep the outfit, though," Nikki said. "It suits you."

"Thanks for reminding me. Mom wants her shoes back I borrowed. See you guys, later."

CHAPTER 39

Blossom was soaking in the Florida sun thinking about Cindy and Jason. They had treated her like family, something she never had growing up in the orphanage and foster care. She thought of her days at St. Agnes when the Sisters told her she probably wouldn't be adopted because of her red hair. People don't like red hair, they told her. People with red hair are dangerous. She was adopted, though, when she was fourteen, by an elderly childless couple. At least they sent her to college even if they were more like prison guards than parents. Her mother died first, and then he died a few months later when Blossom was twenty. She cried at their funerals. There was no one else to cry for them. She wondered where they had come from, but she had never thought to ask them much about themselves. She knew of no one to contact. She inherited the property which was valued at two hundred thousand, but it went for about a hundred thousand at an auction for taxes. She bought a car and her trailer with the money, and still had a little socked away in a savings account.

With the music playing and tanned bodies dancing and swimming, fun was the order of the day. She worked days and had most evenings free. Benny liked her, and she liked him. She was the concierge, and, also, in charge of booking entertainment. That was something she could sink her teeth into. She, also, learned to bartend and helped out when someone called in sick. She felt like it was a set-back at first, but booking entertainment made up for the less desirable aspects. Bennie was a very successful businessman. She could learn a lot from him.

She wore clothes at her concierge job, but whenever she bartended she didn't. Her hair was long enough to cover her breasts, and she wore a wrap around her waist that covered her bottom. After a few weeks of seeing so many naked people she became acclimated. She noticed that most of the naturalists were into aromatherapy and wore a lot of strong perfumes which caused her to sneeze. She thought she would have to get an allergy medication.

Benny was from Florida, and he had a chain of juice gyms besides the resort. He and Blossom hadn't had sex. He considered Blossom an asset and didn't want to jeopardize their relationship. He enjoyed being seen with her, though. Blossom liked Benny, but she felt the same way about him.

He stopped by her concierge desk in the afternoon and asked if she had booked the band he wanted for the dance.

"Yes," she said.

"At the price we discussed?"

"Yes. No problem," she said.

"Okay. Good. I have to go out of town for a few days. Do you want to come with me?"

"Where?" she asked.

"Savannah. I have to buy a couple new treadmills. There are wholesale outlets in Savannah. Go ahead and make Hotel reservations for next Wednesday and Thursday night."

Blossom looked at him a little puzzled.

"Get a suite if you want, or adjoining rooms," he said. "You can help me shop for the machinery."

"Okay," she said.

"I'll see you later," he said.

He was wearing a linen suit jacket with jeans and a cotton shirt without a tie. He always looked so cool, naked or clothed, Blossom thought as he walked away. People were playing ping pong on the patio as music filled the area. It was a nice place to work, and there wasn't the pressure like she had working for Jack. She thought about Cindy and wondered how she was doing and thought she would give her a call soon, but by the following Wednesday she still hadn't called Cindy or she may have known that there was talk that Blossom was a suspect in Jack's murder.

The next week on Wednesday morning Blossom came to the restaurant for breakfast where she was to meet Benny. She was sitting in the corner drinking a pina colada when he arrived a few minutes late. He walked over to her table and pulled out a chair and sat down.

"Good morning. Have you ordered anything to eat?" he asked.

"Just this," she said and indicated the drink.

The waitress came over to the table to take his order.

"Good morning, Marcie," he said.

"Good morning, Benny," she said. "What will you have this beautiful day?"

"I'm going to have my usual over-easy with toast and orange juice and coffee."

"Right away, Sir," she said. "Anything else for you, Blossom?"

"I'll have a toast with honey, please, and coffee. That's all," she said.

Benny picked up his napkin and folded it and unfolded it, and moved it to the other side. He pulled at his collar and unbuttoned it down to the center of his chest. He glanced at Blossom and then looked down and picked the napkin back up then placed it on his lap and cleared his throat. He finally looked her in the eye and spoke.

"Blossom, an FBI agent called me yesterday and asked about you in connection with Jack Higgins' murder."

"What?" she asked.

"I got a call from an FBI agent yesterday. He wanted to know how long you have been working here."

"Really? Is that all they asked you?" she asked.

"Basically," he said. "I didn't realize there had even been a murder. When did that happen?"

"Right before I drove down here. He got shot around midnight leaving the bar at the Hotel. I didn't tell you? I thought I had," she said.

"No, you didn't. I hadn't heard anything about it. Were you and Jack having some kind of problem?"

"No, we weren't having a problem at all. His wife actually asked me to leave," she said, "after she got back from Florida. She wanted her old job back, and I didn't want to go back to housekeeping. Do you think I should call them back?"

"There was no message. They just wanted to know when you started to work here."

"I left right after his funeral. I didn't go to it, and I didn't kill him," she said.

"I sure hope not," Benny said.

"Maybe I should have stayed, but that was kind of like the last straw. I was trying to make up my mind whether to move, and then that happened. I was in shock. I think I'll call my friend, Cindy, my neighbor at the trailer park. I should give her a call. I'll be back in a few minutes. Okay?"

"Okay."

Cindy left the restaurant and went to her room and made the call to Cindy. She was still at home that morning.

"Hi, Cindy," Blossom said.

"Hey, Blossom. How are you doing?"

"I'm alright. I have a quick question for you. Are you busy?"

"No. I was just having a cup of coffee before going to the office."

"The FBI called Benny and asked when I came to work here. I was wondering if anyone had asked you anything about me," she said.

"An FBI agent was at the hotel one day and came into the office and asked if I knew whether you were home the night of the murder, and I said you were. I saw your car parked at home that night."

"I'm glad to hear that. If I were the FBI, I'd be looking at Booboo," she said. "She's the one with motive."

"I heard she hired an investigator," Cindy said.

"That scared me when Benny told me that. My heart started pounding out of my chest. I have to go. I'll talk to you later, Cindy. I miss you guys. Tell Jason hello for me."

"I will. We miss you, too," Cindy said.

"Let me know if you hear anything else, please," Blossom said.

"Okay, but I'm sure it's nothing to worry about," Cindy said.

"I'll talk to you later, Cindy. I have to get going. Bye for now," she said and hung up.

When she and Benny arrived in Savannah everything seemed fine, and they were leaving their suite to have dinner. Benny said they were having dinner with some friends of his. They met them at the restaurant.

"Blossom, these are old and dear friends of mine, Ted and Mary George," he said.

"Hello, Blossom. It's nice meeting you," Mary said.

They sat and had dinner and a few glasses of wine. Benny liked to brag about his successes. Blossom thought maybe he was trying too hard. Ted seemed very interested, though, and asked question after question, but Blossom was bored and started getting sleepy. She asked to be excused and got up to go to the ladies room. Mary said she needed to go, also.

"How long have you been with Benny?" she asked.

"I just met him not long ago, and I moved here to work with him about a month ago."

"Do you like it?" she asked.

"Yes, it's a good job. We are not an item, though," Blossom said. "He wants to keep our relationship on a professional basis."

"Is that what he told you?" she asked and smiled putting on a fresh coat of lipstick as they stood in the bathroom talking.

"Not in so many words, but that's the way it is," she said.

"I think he likes you," she said. "I'm so horny. Do you ever just feel so horny you can't stand it?"

"Sometimes I feel that way, when I'm alone and have no one," she said. "I think about it all the time until I can get me some."

"Yes! Exactly," she said.

They walked back to the table where Benny and Ted were still talking.

"We were beginning to wonder if we were going to have to send a posse for you girls. Will you come up to our suite for a nightcap?" he asked Mary and Ted.

"I suppose we could have one," Mary said.

When they got to their suite Mary and Ted immediately started taking off their clothes, and Benny followed.

"I'm sorry, guys," Blossom said, "but I have a headache. I need to lie down."

"I have some aspirin," Benny said. "Let me get you a couple."

He went into the bathroom and brought her a glass of water and a couple aspirin.

She took the aspirin and said goodnight. Benny didn't like it, but he didn't say much. She walked to her room and locked her door and went to bed. She could hear them making love together, and she felt betrayed for reasons she didn't understand.

CHAPTER 40

I t was Helen's turn to drive for property inspection. Cindy, Irene, John and Mark all got into her car for the grand tour.

"First stop, Jack's Gym," Helen said.

"I haven't seen it before. Where is it?" Cindy asked.

"It's on the other side of the tracks on Riverside," Mark said.

"We'll see it first, then the residential listings," Helen said.

John lit up a joint and passed it around as they drove to the gym.

"Do you think Dottie and Bob smoke pot?" Mark asked.

"They'd never tell," John said.

"Do you think they're screwing?" Mark asked.

"They'd never tell," John repeated.

"I think Dottie and her old man are getting a divorce," Helen said.

"What is Booboo saying about the investigation into who killed Jack," John asked.

"Nothing so far. She said she was watching a movie and went to bed around midnight the night Jack got killed. She said it wasn't anything unusual for Jack to stay out all night, but for some reason she was anxious and had nightmares. She said she was dreaming that Jack was standing in front of her and then just passed through her like the wind. She said it felt terrible, and as soon as she heard the knock on the door and it woke her up, she knew Jack was dead."

"Does she have any ideas about who may have killed him?" Mark asked.

"No. She said he never talked to her about much of anything. She said she thought it was kind of suspicious that Blossom left town in such a hurry, though."

"Blossom was home that night," Cindy said. "Her lights were out, and her car was home when I went to bed around midnight," Cindy said. "She didn't blame Jack. Booboo is the one who fired her, not Jack. He even gave her severance pay. Blossom said Booboo is the one with motive, not her."

"True," John said.

"Well, here it is," Helen said.

They pulled up in the parking lot and parked. It was just a big old cinderblock building with a metal roof and a pair of boxing gloves painted on the wall.

"There's punching bags and a boxing ring, and a basketball hoop, and some weight-lifting equipment," Helen said. "There's an old jukebox with lots of old records. It's probably worth something, and a cigarette machine, and a pop machine."

"Someone will get in there and rob the place," John said.

"It's got steel windows, and it's padlocked," Helen said. "I have the key to it if anyone wants to see inside."

A police car drove by slowly watching them. John pulled out a can of spray and sprayed down the car. Cindy coughed and waved her hands.

"Jesus, that smells even worse than skunkweed. What is that?" Cindy asked.

"It's Hawaiian," he said. "Just in case they stop and ask us what we're doing."

"We're getting a suntan, Officer," Mark said.

They laughed.

"There's a police station right up the road," Helen said.

"How many square feet is it?" Cindy asked.

"It's over five thousand square feet, a hundred and fifty by thirty-five feet. It has a couple gas heaters attached to the ceiling," Helen said. "There's a shower room with a couple toilets. It's in fairly good condition. Does anyone want to go inside?"

"I don't need to see the inside," Cindy said.

"No," Mark and John echoed.

Helen turned around and pulled back out onto the road just as the cop car came back around the bend and followed them down the road for about a mile.

"John, have you heard who may have killed Jack?" Helen asked.

"I heard Pro Bates had him knocked off," John said.

"Pro Bates?" Cindy asked.

"Peter Bates," John said.

"I've never heard of him," Cindy said. "What does he do?"

"He has Jelly's Bread factory," Mark said. "We all love Jelly's Bread."

"I don't," Cindy said. "I don't like bread or milk. I haven't drunk milk since I was a baby."

"Aren't you afraid you'll blow away?" Mark asked.

"I drink chocolate milk sometimes, and I eat grilled cheese sandwiches sometimes, not very often, though."

"Are you allergic?" Helen asked.

"I'm allergic to metals and chemicals. I think I might be lactose intolerant, though.

I eat ice cream and then fart like a freight train."

"I notice that, too," Helen said.

Cindy looked at her like what did you say.

"I mean I do, too, when I eat ice cream," Helen said.

"I thought you meant you'd heard me fart before," Cindy said and laughed.

"I have heard you fart before," Mark said.

"You have not," Cindy said and laughed. "I was diagnosed with MSS, Metals Sensitivity Syndrome. I have to get the fillings removed from my teeth. I have to use all-natural products for cleansers."

"When did you find out?" Helen asked.

"A couple of weeks ago. I'm not supposed to chew gum until I get them out. My doctor said chewing gum releases the gases in the fillings which cause the allergic reaction. I have an appointment in a couple weeks to get them replaced. Also, he said I probably need to move away from the power plant."

"Are you going to?" Helen said.

"I'd like to buy a little house somewhere. I'm just waiting until the right one comes along."

"What price range?" John asked.

"Cheap price range," she said. "I don't want to have to do a lot of work on it, though."

"I just listed a little house over on Chelsey Drive. It's only $60,000. It's nice and clean as a pin," he said. "It's got all wood floors and a stone fireplace. The kitchen is small with a nook, two bedrooms and a den. There's a chain link fence and a doggie door, too."

"Is there a garage?" she asked.

"There's a covered parking pad behind the house off an alley. We're going to go see it." John said.

"Do you want to go see that one next?" Helen asked.

"Let's see the one on Franklin, then we can go to Chelsey," John said.

"What number is the one on Franklin?" she asked.

"It's on the corner of Virginia, one hundred," he said.

"I went to college with Peter Bates," Helen said. "He was always a little prick. Who said he had Jack knocked off?"

"One of the guys," John said. "He supposedly owed Jack a gambling debt. That's what I heard."

They drove to Virginia and turned on Franklin Street. It was a big corner lot with pine trees all down one side of the property. On the other side of the house was a driveway to an attached garage.

"That's nice. How much is it?" Helen asked.

"A hundred and twenty," Mark said.

"Anyone want to go inside?" Helen asked.

"I do," John said. "I have someone who wants a home office."

Helen pulled off the street in front, and they walked up some steps to the front door and knocked. A woman came to the door in curlers and her pajamas.

"We're with Jackson and Greene," Mark said.

"Come on in," she said. "You'll have to excuse my pajamas. My husband had a late flight back from Pittsburg last night so we were late getting to bed."

"No problem. We are all used to seeing folks in their pajamas," John said.

"This is the foyer, of course," she said, "and the living room. This room is small so I keep the treadmill in here and a television. Upstairs we have three bedrooms and a bath and a half. On through here is the kitchen."

They all followed her as she showed them through the house.

"Here is the dining room," she said. "We put up a door here because we don't use it as a dining room. I grade papers here mostly, and have my sewing machine in here. We've started packing so excuse the mess."

"Are you moving to Pittsburg?" Helen asked.

"Yes. My husband got a job at a corporate law firm there. I teach school, and it may be awhile before I get another position. I'm hoping it won't be too long, though."

"What class did you teach?" John asked.

"I teach fifth graders. Here is a bathroom. This is the back door that goes out onto the porch and a patio. The basement stairs are here. My husband uses it for an office, and that's where the laundry room is and the furnace."

"Do you mind if I look in the basement?" John asked.

"No. Just be careful on the stairs. Here's the light switch," she said and flipped the switch.

John opened the door to the basement and walked down the steps as Cindy, Mark and Helen opened the back door and looked outside.

"Is it alright if we look upstairs?" Mark asked.

"Sure. I'll walk up first and make sure my husband is decent," she said.

They waited for her to tell them to come on up then proceeded upstairs.

"My husband is in the shower," she said.

They walked into the master bedroom, and she opened the bathroom door and peeped in then opened the door. The steam from the shower had fogged up the mirror and the shower door. She closed the door quickly.

"We'll have to wait on my husband," she said.

"That's okay," Helen said.

They walked back out into the hallway, and she closed the door and walked on to the other bedrooms.

"The boys' bedrooms have a half-bath with an entry from either side."

She opened the doors and showed them the other bedrooms, then they all walked back downstairs.

"When will you be out of the house?" Cindy asked.

"The middle of next month."

"Thanks for showing us," Cindy said.

"Not at all," she said.

"Good luck with your new home," Helen said. "Is it okay if we look around outside?"

"Sure," she said.

They walked back out the front door and around to the garage and looked, then walked around to the outside basement door and saw John standing in the doorway.

"We almost forgot about you, John," Mark said.

"Come, Pilgrims," John said.

"What the fuck, John," Mark said. "Do we look like fucking Pilgrims?"

"Have some respect," John said.

"Fuck John Wayne," Mark said.

"I was named after John Wayne," he said.

"Your mother named you John Wayne?"

"My dad named me John Wayne Carpenter."

"He should have his head examined," Mark said. "Just stop calling me pilgrim. I don't like it."

"Boys, boys," Helen said. "Shut the fuck up or you can both walk."

They walked back to the car and drove away.

"That was a nice house," Cindy said.

"I doubt if they get that much for it, though," Mark said.

"That's what I was thinking. I would guess it'll sale for about ninety thousand," John said.

"That sounds about right," Mark said.

They pulled up to the house on Chelsea. It had pale green siding, and the cinderblock foundation which was painted black as well as the trim on the porch and the shutters.

"That's different," Cindy said.

"It has a new shingle roof, and there's an outside water line. The porch has outside lights on each side of the door, and there's a street light in the alley," John said.

They all got out of the car and walked to the front door and used the lockbox key to open the door.

"Did the owner die in here?" Cindy asked.

"No. She's in a nursing home. She's ninety-three and still in pretty good health, but her daughter said she's starting to get forgetful, and she was afraid she'd leave something on the stove and catch the house on fire."

They walked inside noticing the plastered walls and the fireplace which had a gas insert and gas logs.

"Is that all the heat there is?" Cindy asked.

"No. It has central gas furnace and air-conditioning. See," John said and pointed to the vents. "There's another gas heater in the bathroom. You could take that insert out if you wanted a wood-burning fireplace. You'd have to clean the chimney, though."

They walked through to the kitchen. The appliances were all white and the cabinets were stained wood. The floor was ceramic tile, and, also behind the sink there was ceramic tile.

"There's a built-in oven and gas range," John said. "The refrigerator looks new."

"Do all the appliances work?" Cindy asked.

"Yes," John said.

There was a hallway off the kitchen to the bedrooms and bathroom. Behind the kitchen was the den.

"You could use this room as a dining room or a den or whatever."

"I like the breakfast nook," Cindy said looking out the bay window. "Jason would love to have a dog."

"There's the doggie door," John said and pointed to the dog door in the den.

"I'll think about it," Cindy said.

One the way back to the office after seeing a few more new listings everyone was anxious to go back inside to make calls to prospective clients. They walked into the office and sat down at their desks and quickly dialed their prospects for the new listings. Cindy called Peter Bates at Jelly's Bread.

"Hello, Mr. Bates. I'm Cindy Hart with Jackson and Greene Realtors. I was wondering if you'd be interested in a new listing we have for Jack's Gym," she said.

CHAPTER 41

Booboo and her cat, Miki, were sleeping late snuggled in her king-size bed with satin sheets when she suddenly woke up to the sound of something like dishes clashing together.

She jumped up out of bed and startled Miki who jumped up and ran under the bed and hid. Booboo opened the nightstand drawer and pulled out a pistol. She peered out the bedroom door into the hallway and walked slowly through the house looking into each room as she passed until she got to the kitchen. There was nothing out of place, but then she noticed the back door wasn't quit shut. She walked outside and looked around, then came back into the house and closed the door. She decided to call the police.

"I think someone was inside my home when I awoke this morning. I heard something and the back door was open. I'm sure I locked it. No," she said, "it doesn't look like anything is missing or broken."

She went back into the bedroom and ran a comb through her hair and pulled on a pair of jeans and a top.

"I think we overslept, Miki," she said. "Come on out."

The cat slowly peered out from under the bed.

"Come on, let's get something to eat," she said and the cat followed her to the kitchen.

The cop was standing at the back door when she walked into the kitchen and scared her again. She jumped, and the cat ran and slid every which way until found another hiding place.

"You scared me!" she said as she opened the door for the young officer.

"I'm sorry. I'm Officer Drake," he said. "Is this the door which was left open?"

"Yes. I heard a loud sound, and it woke me up, but I didn't find anything out of place. Could you look around with me again, please?"

"I looked around outside. I didn't see anything. Do you have a safe or someplace you keep valuables?" he asked.

"It's in my bedroom," she said.

"Did you check to see if anything is missing?" he asked.

"No."

"Let's take a look through the house and in the safe," he said.

They walked back to the bedroom, and Booboo moved a painting aside to reveal a safe which she opened. Officer Drake watched as she picked up jewelry and opened a box which looked like more jewelry and saw a few piles of cash.

"Everything is still here," she said.

"Maybe a bird hit a window or a mouse trap tripped."

"That's possible. My husband was always setting traps, but I don't know where they are."

"You'll smell it," he said.

They walked back through the house as Booboo opened all the closets and looked under the beds as they made their way back to the kitchen. She even opened the kitchen cabinets and looked but didn't see anything amiss.

"I just can't believe I left that door open. Would you like a cup of coffee?" she asked.

"No, thank you. Don't you have a security system? You're very secluded back in here."

"We did, but my husband didn't pay the fee while I was in Florida during the winter," she said. "I need to have it reconnected. I just haven't gotten around to it. Thanks for coming so quickly."

"You're welcome. Is there anything else I can do for you?" he asked politely.

Booboo looked at him and smiled despite herself. He was a nice looking guy.

"You're welcome to stay for a cup of coffee, or tea, or orange juice," she said.

"No, thank you."

The officer didn't move to leave for a few seconds, though. It was hard to turn away from her. He would have loved to stayed, but he was still on probation from his last offense with a woman who called and told on him. He still couldn't figure that one out. She seemed so pleased.

Booboo watched as he got back in his cruiser and drove away.

"Come, Miki," she yelled out. "Here kitty, kitty."

Booboo sat at the counter and drank a cup of coffee. She then fixed the cat's bowl of food and water and walked back to take a shower. Suddenly she was filled with dread. She'd forgotten to look in the shower stall. A clear soap dish shaped like a rose was on the floor. As the shower door opened to reveal her killer Beulah Higgins stood there frozen to the floor feeling nothing but her last breath leaving her body.

CHAPTER 42

Helen was very upset over the news of Booboo's murder. She wondered if Helen's daughter, Nicki would continue with the listings for sale or how that would work, but she hoped Nicki would still want to sale, and if anything may be interested in selling the house, too.

"I don't think there will be any problem with continuing the listings," Helen said. "Of course, I'll have to talk with Nicki."

"Is that her daughter?" Cindy asked.

"Yes. I saw her at Jack's funeral, and now this. It's terrible."

"Where does she live?" Cindy asked.

"She lives in Florida, near Tampa," Helen answered.

"Does she know you listed the hotel and gym?"

"I'm not sure."

"Let me know," Cindy said. "I'm supposed to show the gym to Mr. Bates."

"Who?" John asked.

"Mr. Bates."

"Peter Bates?" John asked incredulously.

"Yes," Cindy said. "I thought if he owed Jack money, he may want to pay it forward."

"Are you serious?" John asked.

"Why not?" Cindy said.

"He's a dangerous man, Cindy. I would have thought you'd learned your lesson," Helen said.

"What do you mean by that? He's never even been arrested. I looked into it. I'm a real estate agent, not a judge and jury."

"You looked into it how?" John asked.

"I made inquiries," Cindy said. "He doesn't have an arrest record."

"I think we should wait and see before going any further," Mark said.

"That's what I said… so let me know," Cindy said

The others rolled their eyes and could barely believe what Cindy had done.

"Was Mr. Bates interested?" Helen asked.

"He said he'd think about it," Cindy said.

"Okay. I'll let everyone know as soon as I know," Helen said.

"Have you thought anymore about the listing on Chelsea, Cindy?" Mark asked.

"I would like to talk with my folks about it this weekend and take Jason to see it," she said.

"Okay. I don't expect it to be on the market long."

"I know. It's a nice little house," Cindy said. "Where is Irene?"

"She's on vacation," John said.

"I can't get over someone killing Mrs. Higgins, in her own home in broad daylight," Helen said. "Can you imagine having someone attack you like that in your own home?"

Cindy looked into the office of the manager. Joe and Dottie stood like they were about to leave but then sat back down as the conversation apparently picked back up. She saw a cat curl up under Dottie's chair.

"What's a cat doing in here," Cindy said.

"What cat?" Helen asked.

"In Bob's office."

"Where?" John asked.

"Under Dottie's chair," Cindy said.

The others were looking, but didn't see anything. Suddenly Cindy realized she must be seeing things again.

"I guess it's a shadow," she said. "It looked just like a cat for a minute. I think I need glasses."

She got up and put her things together and left the office.

Helen, John and Mark looked at each other and shook their heads in astonishment.

"I think Cindy has smoked too much of the wacky weed," Mark said.

"She's lost her fucking marbles if you ask me," Helen said.

CHAPTER 43

Booboo was well-liked among her peers and a respected member of the community even if her husband wasn't. Nicki and her husband and their daughter stood as Helen made her way through the long line at the funeral. Helen briefly expressed her condolences. The service was brief, and Helen decided to attend the graveside services as well.

The dirt on Jack's grave was still freshly dug. Nicki wept with a broken heart as a song was sung in remembrance. As everyone walked away from the gravesite Helen approached Nicki and wrapped her arm around her.

"I'm so sorry for your loss, Nicki. I don't know if you remember me, but I've known your mother and dad for many years," she said.

Nicki was somewhat taken aback. She didn't know Helen.

"I'm sorry, but I don't," Nicki said.

"You sure look like your mother," Helen said engagingly. "Booboo gave me the listing on the hotel and gym recently. I suppose you will want to continue with the sale of the property."

"I suppose so," Nicki said. "I have an appointment with the attorney tomorrow."

Helen handed her business card to Nicki and cupped her hand around it.

"Please let me know as soon as possible. We have interested parties," she said.

"Of course," Nicki said. "I'll call you."

They all walked away as Helen drew a deep breath and exhaled, mission accomplished.

CHAPTER 44

After Blossom and Benny got back to Miami, Blossom didn't feel the same. She felt depressed. Perhaps the death of Jack had finally sunk in. Benny is just a pervert, she thought. She couldn't stop crying. When Cindy called the next morning Blossom was surprised and happy to hear from her.

"Hey, Cindy! I've been thinking of calling you. You must've read my mind," Blossom said.

"How are you?" Cindy asked. "I didn't wake you did I?"

"No, I was awake, just lying around killing time. I thought this place would pick me up, and it did for a while, but now it's kind of boring. How are you all doing?"

"We're all good, except for Mrs. Higgins," she said.

"What's wrong with her?"

"She was murdered," Cindy said.

"What did you say?"

"Mrs. Higgins was found in her home shot to death," Cindy said.

"You're kidding!"

"No. It happened Monday morning."

"Do they know who did it?"

"I don't think so."

"It was probably the same person that killed Jack," Blossom said.

"That's what I was thinking," Cindy said.

"What the hell is going on?" Blossom asked.

"I'm sorry," Cindy said.

"That's okay," Blossom said. "It's not your fault."

"Maybe I should have lead up to it better than that," Cindy said.

"I'm just glad I'm in Florida and have an alibi!"

"Yes, me, too!" Cindy said. "I was on property inspection."

"Is anyone saying who they think may have done it or anything?" Blossom asked.

"No. Helen said everyone is completely at a loss. She listed the hotel and the gym after Jack died. She'll probably list the house, too, now."

"Maybe it was some gangster type. They were always accusing Jack and Chuck. Have you heard anything else from Chuck?"

"No. We agreed not to see each other anymore."

"I know, but I just thought maybe he'd called. Can you call him?"

"No, I can't," Cindy said.

"I wonder who will run the hotel now. Maybe I should call Nicki and tell her I'm available. I wonder what she would say. I wonder if she heard anything about me and Jack."

"I doubt it. You could tell her you have worked there and were filling in for her mom while she was in Florida, that you have experience. She could do no more than say no."

"I might just do that," Blossom said.

"I should get off here," Cindy said. "I'm using the office phone."

"Okay. Thanks for letting me know, Cindy."

"I'll talk to you later," Cindy said and hung up.

"Are you going to your folks this weekend, Cindy?" John asked.

"Yes," she answered. "Jason will be coming back with me. School starts next week."

"That's right! Where has the summer gone?"

"This has been the shortest summer," Mark said.

"Let's go to the river this afternoon. Who's with me?" Cindy asked.

"That sounds like a great idea," Mark said.

"In my Dockers?" John asked.

"You wear boxers, don't you?" Mark asked.

"Yes, but they have holes in them," John said.

"We could go home and get our swimming suits on and pick up a lawn chair," Cindy said.

"I'm ready. I have fishing poles and a couple lawn chairs in my trunk. We can stop by your house, John," Mark said.

John closed his book and put his things inside his briefcase.

"Helen, do you want to go to the river with us this afternoon?" John asked her.

She was still on the phone and shook her head no.

"Well, let's get this show on the road," John said.

"If anyone calls," Cindy said to the secretary, "tell them we went to Mexico."

"Mexico!" the secretary said and laughed. "Okay, but don't drink too many margaritas!"

Helen hung up the phone and looked around at the empty desks. The secretary was on the phone talking to her boyfriend and laughing, oblivious to Helen. She closed her books and waited until the secretary hung up.

"Joyce," she said. "Can you call Mrs. Higgins house and see if her daughter answers. If she answers, ask her when it would be convenient for us to get together."

"What is her daughter's name?" she asked.

"Nicki," Helen answered.

Joyce dialed the number, and Nicki answered the phone.

"Nicki, this is Joyce with Jackson and Greene Realtors. When would it be convenient for you to talk with Helen, our listing agent?"

Helen waited to hear what Joyce would say next.

"Yes, she's here."

Joyce held her hand over the phone and spoke to Helen.

"She wants to know if she can come by here in a little while."

"Yes, that would be great."

"She will be here. Alright, thank you, Nicki."

Joyce hung up the phone.

"She said she'll be here in about a half an hour," she said.

"Good," Helen said. "Thank you, Joyce."

Helen walked into the lobby and over to the concierge.

"Hi, Danny. How are you?"

"Fit as a fiddle," he said. "How are you, Helen?"

"I'm waiting on Nicki. I hope she doesn't pull my listings."

"Do you have a buyer for the hotel?" he asked.

"No, but I haven't even advertised it yet. I think it's a good deal for the right party. Do you have an ashtray?" she asked.

"Yes. I keep one in my desk drawer."

He pulled out the ashtray and put it on the desk.

"Thanks. I don't want to be standing outside when Nicki comes, like I'm waiting on the bus or something."

Helen lit up a cigarette and took a draw and blew it out. Suddenly she glanced back down at Danny's hand. He was wearing a gold band on his little finger. She observed tiny scratches on it.

"Did you get married, Danny?" she said looking at the ring.

"No. I found it in the hallway," he said.

"Oh," she said.

She took another puff off her cigarette then stubbed it out.

"Thanks, Danny," she said.

He emptied the ashtray into the waste can and put it back in his drawer. Helen's eye was drawn to the ring again. She walked back to her office and waited on Nicki.

CHAPTER 45

Cindy and the guys were sitting on lawn chairs with water up to their knees drinking beer. John and Mark were fishing, and Cindy was smoking a joint. It was quiet except for the chirping of birds.

"I wonder what's going to happen with the hotel," John said.

"Do you think we'll find a buyer?" Mark said.

"I don't know. We have to or the State will step in and take it," John said.

"I don't think they owed that much on it," Mark said.

"It won't matter if they don't have the cash," John said.

"I wonder about the gym," Cindy said. "Who is going to buy that big cow."

"Pro Bates, maybe," John said.

"Maybe. I hope whoever buys the hotel doesn't kick us out," Cindy said.

"Me, too. It's definitely a good location for a real estate business," Mark said.

"My sales have doubled since we've been there," John said.

"Mine, too," Cindy said.

"I wonder if the cops have any leads," Mark said.

"I haven't heard a thing," Cindy said.

"Me, neither," Mark said.

"If it weren't for Mrs. Higgins getting murdered, I don't think they'd give a shit about who killed Jack," John said.

"Who would have thought our landlords would both be dead before our one-year lease was up," Cindy said.

"Strange," John said.

"Do you ever wonder what Bob and Dottie and Joe are talking about in there all the time?" Cindy asked.

"I think Bob and Dottie are having an affair, and Joe covers for them," Mark said.

"Really?" Cindy asked.

"I don't know. They sure have a lot to talk about, though," Mark said.

"They sure do. They're like the three musketeers or something," Cindy said.

"I still say Blossom shot Jack," Mark said.

"I don't think Blossom would do anything like that," Cindy said.

"You never can tell about people," John said.

They sat on the river for a couple hours until the beer was gone, and Mark caught a fish. No one wanted it, though, so he threw it back in, and they got up and pulled in their lines and folded their chairs and walked back to the car.

CHAPTER 46

Conversation flowed easily between Helen and Nicki as they discussed the problem of her estate now. To Helen's relief, Nicki had no intentions of keeping the hotel or the gym.

"I don't know want anything to do with it. I have my life with my husband and daughter in Florida, and Phil isn't going to move up here, that's for sure. The attorneys and the CPA can keep the business afloat until we can arrange for the sale," Nicki said.

Joyce interrupted with an announcement.

"Helen, there's a call for you," Joyce said. "It's Blossom."

"Do you mind if I take this call? It's one of the girls who used to work here. I'll just be one minute."

"No, go ahead," Nicki said.

Helen answered mostly out of curiosity, and Nicki turned around in her chair then stood up and took a few steps away to give her some privacy.

"Hello, Blossom. How may I help you?" Helen said.

It was quiet for a minute while Blossom talked to Helen.

"Yes. I see. I'll give her the message. Okay," Helen said and wrote down a number and hung up.

"That was Blossom Moses. She asked me to give you her number.

She said to call her if she could possibly get her old job back. She worked in housekeeping for a few years then Mr. Higgins promoted her to Human Resource Manager while Mrs. Higgins was in Florida."

"That might not be a bad idea," Nicki said. "Did she do a good job?"

"I think it was Blossom's idea to lease out this space to our company and to hire a concierge. I don't think Mrs. Higgins was completely happy with the concierge, though."

"This is a Florida number, isn't it?" Nicki asked.

"Yes. She got a job at a nudist resort in Tampa, but she said she's homesick and wants to come back."

"A nudist resort? Wow. How old is she?"

"I would guess in her late thirties."

"Do you have any ideas about who could have killed my parents?" Nicki asked.

Helen shook her head no and sighed. Nicki looked over at the concierge desk and watched Danny for a minute. He was wearing purple again.

"I could swear he is wearing your mother's wedding band," Helen said. "I know they're all alike, but hers had scratches on it. I remember noticing that one day at the beauty shop, and I asked her about it because it looked like an engraving. She said she'd dropped it and got it scuffed up. He said he found it in the hallway."

"Seriously?" Nicki asked.

"I asked him if he'd gotten married," Helen said. "He's gay."

"Mom wasn't wearing her wedding band when they found her, and I haven't found it. I hadn't thought much about it. Her diamond was in the safe. The cop said everything looked like it was when she was checking it out earlier in the morning. If someone had gotten into the safe, they'd have taken the cash and the diamond. She didn't wear the diamond everyday like she did her wedding band. She always wore her wedding band, though," Nicki stuttered on the verge of tears.

"Mrs. Higgins was going to let him go," Helen said.

"That's motive," Nicki said. "But what about Dad? Why would he kill Dad?"

"I don't know, but I think the two are unrelated," Helen said.

"What makes you think that?" Nicki asked.

"Intuition," Helen said. "Mr. Higgins approved of Danny. He didn't have any problem with Danny. Maybe Danny thought your mother killed him, and he thought she was going to fire him, so he killed her."

"Mom may have been angry with Dad, but she didn't kill him. She was devastated."

"Yes, she was. It broke my heart to see her that way."

"I'm going to report that to the police. Do you think it would be a good idea to hire back Blossom?" she asked.

"I couldn't say. The CPA would know that better than anyone."

Nicki nodded her head in agreement.

"Thank you, Helen. I'll be in touch, and you call me anytime if there is anything you need."

Nicki stood to leave, and Helen stood and walked with her to the door to the lobby. They stood looking over at Danny momentarily.

"I wouldn't know what to say to him," Nicki said. "But I am going to relay this information to the authorities. It bears looking into."

"I agree," Helen said. "Thanks for taking the time to come out here today."

"You're welcome. We'll speak again soon," she said.

Danny watched as she walked out into the lobby and toward the front door. He glanced over at Helen who seemed to be glaring at him. He glared back at her and turned his nose to her. He could tell they'd been talking about him.

CHAPTER 47

Nicki had felt ill ever since she heard that Danny was wearing her mother's wedding band. Being at home where her mother was murdered was horrible. The security system was back, and it wasn't that she feared for her own life, but she decided to call the police about Danny. She thought about Blossom and decided, also, to call Blossom first. She wondered how Blossom knew Danny.

"Hello, Blossom. This is Nicki. I'm Jack and Booboo's daughter. Helen gave me the message. I'll be back in Florida in a couple days, and I thought maybe we could get together to discuss it."

Blossom was jumping up and down she was so happy Nicki had called her.

"Yes, I am interested. If I can help in any way, I would be more than happy to do it," she said.

"Another reason I'm calling, Blossom, is that I understand you hired the concierge. Did you know him before, is he a friend of yours?" she asked.

"I didn't know him personally, but he was recommended to me by a mutual friend. I thought a concierge would help the hotel rating, and one of my friends mentioned Danny needed a job. He has a part-time job at the Civic Center in maintenance. We didn't need anyone in maintenance, but if there was an opening, he could maybe get that job full time if the concierge thing didn't work out."

"Did Dad like him?"

"I think so. He called him a fruit, but he liked him, I think. He didn't want him full-time, though. The money we got from the lease to Jackson and Greene more than covered his salary. It would have covered a full-time salary, but Mr. Higgins said only part-time, but later on, maybe he could get full time. I thought if we had an opening in maintenance, he might be happy with that for the benefits."

"What about Mother. Did she like him?"

"She didn't say anything about him to me."

"Did my parents have any significant problems with anyone you know about?" she asked.

"Not really. No one I know disliked them, especially Mrs. Higgins. Everyone liked her, and most people were fond of Mr. Higgins as well. I know I was. He was a good man. I am so sorry all this has happened. It really is so sad."

"Are your parents still living, Blossom?"

"I was adopted when I was fourteen. They were elderly and died when I was twenty."

"Oh, I see. It's terrible to lose both parents especially this way and so close together. I don't think I'll ever get over it."

"I'm so sorry for your loss."

"Thank you."

Nicki cried and tried to regain her composure to continue. It took her awhile to speak again.

"Could we meet for lunch on Saturday? You aren't that far from Tampa, are you?" Nicki asked.

"No, not at all," Blossom said.

"I'll call you Saturday morning around ten o'clock so we can work out the details. Bye for now."

Nicki hung up and thought about what Blossom said. There wasn't much insight regarding Danny, but it didn't matter. She picked up the card off the kitchen counter and called the investigator who was working the case and told him that one of the ladies recognized her mother's wedding band on someone else's finger, the concierge. It was the best news he'd had all day.

"What is the lady's name who recognized the ring?" he asked.

"Helen. She works for Jackson and Greene Realtors. They have an office at the hotel. Helen listed the hotel and my dad's gym for Mom after Dad… she and Mom were acquainted. Helen said she thought it was an engraving on Mom's ring at first, but Mom told her she had dropped it and got it scratched. The concierge told Helen he had found the ring in the hallway. I suppose he may have, so maybe it's nothing, but Mom wore her wedding band all the time I've ever known her. Even when it was scratched, she was still wearing it."

"I'll have him brought in for questioning," he said. "You don't have to worry about that."

"I'm going back to Florida Friday. I'm not sure when I'll be back," she said. "I just wanted to let you know what Helen said."

"Thanks for calling. I'll call you as soon as I know anything."

She already knew what the CPA had to say about the last few months' business at the hotel. It had picked up after a slump when her dad was indicted. Blossom knew the ropes and Nicki was desperate. She needed to get things organized as quickly as possible.

Miki came into the kitchen and wrapped her tail around Nicki's leg purring.

"Do you want to move to Florida, girl," she asked.

She picked her up and sat her on her lap and petted her.

"We'll need to pack your toys, won't we? Yes, we will."

CHAPTER 48

It was only a matter of time until things got back to normal, so to speak. Blossom got her old job back, and Danny was arrested for the murder of Mrs. Higgins. Blossom hired a new concierge, and Cindy surprised even herself when Mr. Bates agreed to buy the old Jack's Gym and turned it into a Jelly's Bread outlet with a convenience store.

Cindy was still having hallucinations, though, and it was unfortunate that Chuck didn't live to see the house she bought or Jason's new dog, a German Shephard pup he called Champ. On the way to the office one morning Cindy heard on the radio that Danny was found guilty. When she walked inside the office everyone was talking about it.

"Did you hear? Danny was found guilty," Helen said.

"I heard it on the radio coming in," Cindy said.

"Chuck and Danny sort of traded places," John said. "I mean Danny is in jail now, and Chuck is dead."

"I suppose, if you think Danny was dead before," Cindy said.

"Who do you think killed Jack?" John asked.

"We may never know," Cindy said.

Blossom walked by the glass window in the lobby and outdoors. She headed for Randy's Seafood wearing a beautiful floral printed dress that showed a lot of cleavage.

"That's what I call well-endowed," Mark said.

"No shit, Pilgrim," John said.

Mark and Cindy shook their heads.

"Have you ever considered moving to Plymouth Rock, John?" Mark asked.

"That possibility had not occurred to me," he said.

"I think we have reciprocal laws, so maybe you should find out about that," Cindy said.

Normal is a relative term. We should all be so lucky. There was no more talk about getting rid of the real estate office at the hotel anyway, thanks to Blossom and the CPA. Numbers don't lie, and even if they could, they wouldn't have any reason.

THE END